WE'LL HAVE A WONDERFUL CORNISH CHRISTMAS

CP WARD

AMMFA
PUBLISHING

For the residents of Tintagel,
who will no doubt be appalled at the liberties
I've taken with their village.

Thank you, and Merry Christmas!

ALSO BY CP WARD

WE'LL HAVE A WONDERFUL CORNISH CHRISTMAS

AN UNEXPECTED VISITOR

LUCY DRAKE SPUN THE BIRO ACROSS THE TOP OF her fingers with the deftness and confidence of a mastered skill. None of the customers browsing the stands of Sunny Day Travel had noticed yet, but they would, sooner or later. She lifted her hand, preparing to repeat the process, when the front door swung open and a man came bundling in, a baby in his arms, with a woman behind him struggling to get a baby stroller through the closing door. As one wheel got stuck on the corner of carpet that was always coming loose, Lucy immediately started to stand. It was an automatic reaction to a common situation, but as she moved for the gap between her desk and Paul's, she glanced once more at the man.

A face accurately described as bland was made no better by a cheap Christmas scarf, two pixilated knitted Father Christmases swinging back and forth across his neck. He frowned at the baby as a chubby hand reached for one line of tassels, making a confident cooing sound as he looked back at the woman. He gave a smug chuckle then muttered, 'Come on, Percival, wait your turn.'

Lucy froze.

Oh no. Not now, please.

'Lucy?'

Melanie, the manager and owner, was staring at her. Already engaging with a client, it left only Lucy or the new guy Paul to deal with this fresh drama before it unfolded.

But Paul was on a break. Lucy glanced at the clock, and her heart sank. Impossible that she could leave the family struggling in the doorway for the four minutes it would take for Paul to return.

Her best chance to avoid the man was to engage with the woman. She hurried around the desk, her head lowered, putting her back to the man as she reached for the door.

'Here, let me help you with that. It's always getting stuck.'

A blast of wind through the open door ruffled her neatly clipped hair. If only Paul was back, she could use it as an excuse to hide—

'Don't worry, I've got it,' the man said, one arm poking into Lucy's line of vision to hold the door. 'Multi-tasking and all that. Not just a skill for women, is it?'

She didn't need to look up to know it was him. She closed her eyes, keeping her head lowered, afraid Dennis Faber would recognise her after all this time.

She had changed a little—dyed her hair and put on a stone—but life had been relatively sedate over the last twelve years. No great dramas or stresses beyond the everyday ones, leaving her no more than an early-thirties version of the girl he had humiliated at their Sixth Form ball.

'There you are,' Lucy said, still not looking up as the stroller's wheel finally came loose. The woman pulled it into the shop and the door mercifully swung shut.

'Thank you very much,' the woman said. 'It's such a struggle getting this thing around sometimes.'

Lucy, keeping her back to Dennis, smiled at her. 'If you're just looking to browse, you'll find all our Christmas deals on the rack here—'

'Oh no, we're ready to reserve,' Dennis said, cutting her off. 'Lapland all the way. Show the little one what Christmas is all about.'

As the smugness in his voice began to grate, Lucy felt an urge to mention her own solo trip to Lapland five years ago, when a power cut had reduced the inclusive Christmas dinner to cold cuts, it had snowed so heavily she had seen nothing out of the roof of her fabled glass-igloo capsule room, and the Northern Lights hadn't shown up. An expensive waste of money, but if that was what they wanted and it would get them out of the shop as quickly as possible—

'Frankie? Frankie, is that you? Oh my God, talk about blast from the past.'

The pain was starting to kick in. Lucy squeezed her eyes closed, steeled herself for the impending horror of a confrontation, then forced a smile and opened them again. She turned to face the first of many boyfriends to dump her.

'Dennis Faber? I'm sorry, I didn't recognise you.'

Dennis gave her a wide, punchable grin and spread his arms. One held the baby like a wrapped sandwich as chubby arms waved in the air.

'Come on, Frankie … or are you going by Frances now? I haven't changed much. Perhaps matured with age, like a fine wine—'

Lucy risked a glance at Melanie's desk, but her older boss's head was down as she talked with a client. With a bit of luck she hadn't overheard.

'Dennis? Is this an old friend?'

The woman wore a frown as she cocked her head in that politely suspicious way Lucy had used herself on occasion when confronted with an ex's former partner.

'School friend,' Lucy said, using the nicest word she could, even though they had never been friends. Confidence-booster might have worked better from her side, pity-shag from his, even though she had never let him get that far. 'And I go by Lucy now.'

'Oh, your middle name? I suppose that makes sense.' Dennis leaned forward. He glanced at his yet-to-be-introduced wife and gave a conspiratorial wink. 'This is the girl I was telling you about,' he said, and Lucy realised she had never felt more like punching someone than now. 'The one who could empty a room in five seconds.' He looked at Lucy. 'Do you still do it? Or have you had it fixed?'

Lucy glowered at him. She suddenly felt sick, and thought it quite possible she would vomit all over his gaudy scarf, Ralph Lauren sweater, and baby Percival too, if she didn't get out of there right away.

A door opened behind her. She glanced back, saw the face of her saviour, eighteen-year-old trainee travel agent Paul, hair greased to his head in one of those post-adolescent hairstyles he still thought was cool.

'Paul will help you,' she gasped, clutching her stomach. 'I'm afraid nature calls.' She glanced at Dennis's wife. 'That time of the month,' she added, giving half a shrug.

'We're back on those too, aren't we?' Dennis said with an embarrassing chuckle. 'After nine months of bliss.'

Lucy wished she had time to slap him as his wife turned to give him a sharp reprimand, but she really had to get out of there before something went wrong. She ran for the STAFF ONLY door and burst through into a little office and kitchen as the muffled sound of Dennis laughing off his wife's anger came from behind her.

Then she was diving through the door into the cubicle toilet and locking it, wishing she could lock out all the stresses of the world at the same time. The situation was so absurd that she wanted to laugh, but she had promised herself on that long ago day when her humiliation had reached its Everest summit, that she would never, ever, *ever*, laugh again.

2

CONFESSIONS

'You know, lying on a C.V. has to be some kind of crime,' Melanie said, handing Lucy a coffee, then lifting an eyebrow and nodding at the sugar bowl as though that would make everything all right. 'So you switched your first and middle names? A good job I'm too lazy to ask for passport copies, isn't it? So your name is Frances Lucy Drake?'

Lucy sighed. 'It gets worse, since this is confession time. It's Frances Lucinda Scullion-Drake. Scullion is my mother's maiden name. Somehow that got me the nickname of Onion Duck in primary school. It only dropped when we started on the Spanish Armada in secondary school history class. Never mattered to the other kids that the male version is spelled differently. I'd get kids I barely knew hollering 'Admiral' or 'man the cannons' at me from the other end of the corridor. I went with Frankie for a while, but that always felt so … eighties.'

Melanie chuckled. 'Could be worse, being named after a historical figure. Melanie Dorothy Jones … pretty boring, don't you think?'

'It's a nice safe name. Francesca was my grandmother's name on my father's side. Apparently, he went with Frances because it was easier to spell.'

Melanie laughed again. 'You must be able to see the funny side. You're good at your job, but you could do with lightening up a little.' Melanie lifted her coffee. 'Anyway, your secret's safe with me. And possibly with Paul, but I don't think he really caught what was going on.'

'Thanks.'

'Have you decided where you're going for Christmas this year?'

'Can't you just keep the shop open? I'll work it on my own if you like.'

Melanie's face turned serious. Lucy had heard the story before, but Melanie looked set to tell it again.

'Absolutely not. My father died of a stroke on December 28th, 2003,' Melanie said, taking a long sip of coffee and then wincing at the heat. 'I wasn't there, because I was working. I worked all that Christmas period, and I vowed I never would again.' She smiled. 'And now this is my shop, so I can do what I like. Doors close December 18th, and I'll see you again on January 2nd. No arguments. And if you pitch a tent outside I'll call the council to come and sweep you away.'

'No chance, then?'

'None. What are your plans? Come on, we can get

some juicy staff discounts. What was it last year? Trekking the Black Forest?'

Lucy shook her head. 'That was two years ago. Last year I walked the Scottish coast path.'

'In the freezing cold? I bet that was fun.'

'I enjoyed it. It didn't snow every day. In fact, mostly it just rained. Must have been the sea air. I was thinking of something a little more Christmassy this year, like doing the Mont Blanc circuit.'

'How will that be Christmassy? Snow alone does not a Christmas make.'

'Well, what do you suggest?'

Melanie grinned. 'Here's a radical idea. Why don't you go and see your family this year? I know I can't force you, but you know what I feel about it….'

Lucy shrugged. 'I went there for Christmas Day last year. I flew out for Scotland on Boxing Day.'

'So you gave them one day of your vacation? How kind of you. You know that goes against my philosophy, and Christmas Day is the worst anyway, because that's when everyone's rushing around trying to get things opened, drunk, cooked, and served. It's the other days that are the best, when you're just lounging around. Why don't you spend a few of those with them?'

Lucy closed her eyes. Other unpleasant memories were coming back. 'I don't like being around too many people,' she said. 'I find it awkward. All that joviality, all that laughter—'

Melanie put down her coffee cup with a sudden bump. 'Look, Lucy, I'll be straight with you. You're a pretty girl. At thirty you're probably not quite as pretty as you were at twenty-two, but you're not on the shelf just yet. You're wasted traipsing through forests over Christmas. You should be with your family, or in the arms of some lusty woodcutter … or is that why you go?' Melanie lifted an eyebrow and flashed a conspiratorial grin. 'What aren't you telling me?'

Lucy gave a violent shake of her head. 'No—'

'Just lighten up a little. You know, I don't think I've ever heard you laugh.'

The conversation was moving into areas Lucy wanted to avoid. 'I think my break's over,' she said.

Melanie rolled her eyes. 'You're not on a break. This is a staff meeting. And as your manager, I'm commanding you to enjoy yourself this Christmas.'

'I like deserted beaches and forests. Perhaps this year I'll go ice-canoeing in the Norwegian fjords, get the best of both worlds.'

'Alone?'

'Of course.'

Melanie shook her head. 'I can see into your head, Lucy Drake.' She lifted her glasses and squinted at Lucy. 'And what I see is a girl running away.'

'I'm not running away. I just like solitude a lot more than I like being around big groups of people, all laughing and trying to get me drunk, and … and laughing….'

'I'll tell you what,' Melanie said. 'Either you spend some quality time with your family this year or I'll change your name tag to Frances Drake and put you in charge of historical holidays.'

'You wouldn't do that, would you?'

Melanie lifted an eyebrow. 'Try me.'

'I'll think about it.'

'Good. Right, we'd better get out there. It sounds like Paul's run off his feet.'

They went back through into the shop and found Paul standing alone by the leaflet rack advertising student holidays to Eastern European cities.

'All right?' he said, turning around. 'Just tidying up.'

'Paul,' Melanie said, 'how do you like to spend your Christmas?'

'With me mates,' Paul said.

'How about family?'

Paul shrugged. 'Depends how much booze the old man has got in.'

Melanie lifted an eyebrow as she turned to Lucy. 'See? Paul likes to spend his holidays with his friends and family.'

Paul looked from one to the other then gave a shrug as though older women were an entirely different and unexplainable species.

'You'll love it,' Melanie said. 'And it'll do you good.'

'I'll think about,' Lucy said with another sigh.

THERAPY

IT WAS A CASUAL INVITATION. MELANIE, FORTY-FIVE and divorced but still attractive in that carefree-but-drinks-a-little-too-much way, would no doubt have the vodka on tap to celebrate her first night of the Christmas holidays, be looking to get laid and ideally get Lucy laid too. She had invited the staff of every retailer on the Clifton Triangle to her townhouse on Clifton Avenue, a three-storey divorce-settlement monstrosity set in its own grounds which she shared only with a geriatric Labrador now that her two adult children were off at university. She had even taken Lucy with her to invite the staff of the new sports shoe store two doors down from the Starbucks, because 'they're all young guys, and once you get some Kahlua punch in them they'll be anybody's.'

Lucy, who had last made the mistake of drinking too much six months ago at an old university friend's party, wasn't keen. She didn't have a specific excuse, so after Melanie had closed the travel agent for the Christmas holidays at lunchtime and gone off to do some last-minute shopping, Lucy wandered up and down Park Street, idly looking through the trendy townie and student shops, half hoping that some chancer would cast her an evening cinema invite on a whim.

While it didn't happen, a three o'clock appointment with her therapist (and aunt) at least gave her a little more thinking time. As Aunt Agatha let her into her second floor flat off Whiteladies Road, Lucy considered just turning off her phone to avoid Melanie's certain hassling in the event of a no-show, and later playing ignorant or blaming a toilet-related accident.

'So, how are we today?' Aunt Agatha—or as patients knew her, Dr. Woakes—asked, settling into the creaking leather swivel chair that looked far more comfortable than the sofa on which Lucy always had to sit.

'Life is a complete nightmare,' Lucy said. 'I'm single, which isn't the problem, but because I'm thirty, everyone I meet thinks it is. I'm supposed to go to a party tonight where I can guarantee someone will try to match-make me, probably with someone inappropriate. I'll get drunk to try to get out of it then humiliate myself. Alternatively, if I'm match-made with someone nice, I'll get drunk to try to relax, and then humiliate myself. Either way, the result is the same.'

'And you can't get out of it because why?'

'Because I don't have an acceptable excuse.'

Aunt Agatha gave a sage nod. 'Melanie's party?'

Lucy nodded.

'It sounds like a right laugh from what you've told me. Didn't you say last year she had a horse?'

'Someone showed up with one, yeah. They just left it chained up in the back garden with Reginald.'

'Who?'

'The dog.'

'Oh.'

'I mean, it was a gimmick, and it sounded cool, but she was scared it would kick someone so no one was allowed near it. People spent most of the evening taking selfies with it out of the living room window. Apart from one guy who tried to serenade it.'

'Did it kick him?'

'Bit his shoulder. He wasn't invited this year, apparently. Although, to be fair, neither was the horse.'

'Why don't you just go?'

'You know why.'

Aunt Agatha sighed. 'You can't spend your whole life being so serious,' she said. 'For better or worse, a good laugh is always worth it.'

'No, it's really not. Even alone it's not.'

For a therapist, Aunt Agatha didn't seem particularly patient, but then Lucy was getting a friends and family rate of precisely zero, on the condition that Lucy recommend her aunt to anyone she knew who had issues.

'Well, I suppose at least you won't get wrinkles.

People look at me and think I'm fifty years older than I am. I tell them I just enjoy a good laugh. So, what's your plan for your Christmas holidays this year?'

Lucy remembered the flyer she had picked up earlier that morning. 'I'm going to walk around Sicily,' Lucy said. 'Just me, a tent, and a backpack.'

'Have you booked your flight yet?'

Lucy shook her head. 'Not yet. There are always last-minute cancellations, and Melanie's always cool with us using the staff card to get a discount.' She looked up as Aunt Agatha smiled. 'Why?'

'It's just that I heard your parents were going on holiday this Christmas,' she said.

'Really? They didn't tell me.'

'Have you asked them?'

Lucy shrugged. 'I haven't spoken to them in two weeks. I keep meaning to call, but at this time of year Mum always makes me her project case.'

'Lucy, I love you as my niece and my sister's only-born, but sometimes you're infuriating.'

'As my therapist, aren't you supposed to support me?'

'Of course, but as your aunt, I'm allowed to tell you when to pull your socks up. Look, you'd better get on the phone quick. They're leaving tomorrow morning.' Aunt Agatha leaned forward and winked. 'And wouldn't that give you a good excuse not to go to Melanie's party?'

Lucy sighed. Part of her felt hurt that her parents had thought of themselves rather than honouring their yearly Christmas dinner when Lucy would reluctantly stop by for a couple of hours during the middle of the day, usually between bouts of solitude. On the other hand, Aunt Agatha was right. She was a rubbish daughter, and had been for as long as she'd been old enough to make her own choices.

'Where are they going?' she asked.

'Cornwall.' Aunt Agatha smiled. 'I can't think of anywhere else I'd rather be at Christmas. In a cozy beachside cottage, with my family … fantastic. Well, except for a cold cliff path in Sicily, getting stared at by goats and weird yokels. Come on, Lucy. You should go with them.'

'They'll still be there next year. Plus, I've always wanted to go to Sicily,' she added, even though it hadn't even occurred to her until a couple of hours ago.

'Have you checked the Italian weather? It'll probably just rain the whole time.' Aunt Agatha gave a handful of papers a professional shuffle and lifted an eyebrow. 'And will your parents still be there next year? Have you asked Melanie for her thoughts on that?'

Lucy looked down. It was hard to defeat the logic when it was presented, but the wall she had built around her fragile confidence often dominated her thoughts. Letting in emotions from outside posed a threat to her personal security.

'You're right,' she said at last. 'I should go with them. It's just … you don't understand how it feels when something bad happens. No one does.'

4

CHRISTMAS PARTY

MELANIE CALLED NINE TIMES BEFORE LUCY FINALLY relented and picked up the phone.

'So, did you manage to come up with an excuse?'

'I'm still working on it. I'm lying in the middle of Gloucester Road, waiting to be run over by a lorry.'

'Come on, Lucy, what are you afraid of? It's Christmas!'

'It's December the seventeenth.'

'Close enough. Come on round. I'm just making the punch. Tescos had Christmas spice on two jars for one so it's got an extra kick this year.'

Lucy held the phone away from her ear to let out a sigh. Then she said, 'Okay, I'll be over in an hour.'

'Glad rags on, girl. It'll be a ratio of three guys for every girl. I conveniently forgot to invite those tarts from the hairdressers next door.'

'It might be fun,' Lucy muttered under her breath

as she waited for a bus down Gloucester Road. 'It might be fun. It might … be fun.'

'Or it might not,' said an old crone standing nearby, reaching up to pat Lucy's arm with one ancient hand. 'If he tells you to take it, just say no. Didn't you ever watch *Grange Hill?*'

Lucy swallowed her confusion long enough to smile. 'Not for twenty years.'

'My grandkids loved it.' Then, grinning, the old woman added, 'If you need a wingman, I'm free tonight. Reg will be watching the game, won't even notice if I'm not there.'

'My friend's dog is called Reg,' Lucy said.

The old bag cackled. 'My Reg ain't much of a dog, not until he gets a couple of pints into him, and then it's all action. Discovery Channel and all that—'

'Here's my bus,' Lucy said hurriedly, stepping away as the bus pulled in. The old woman gave her a crinkled thumbs-up as Lucy climbed on board and sat down, followed by a rather lewd gesture Lucy hoped was just the result of some nervous condition.

It was a relief when the bus pulled away.

Half an hour later, she was walking up Park Street, wondering if she should just give up and go into the no-alcohol bar that had just opened up where the record shop had once been, certain she could avoid finding anything to laugh at. As she passed the windows though, she saw it was playing an old episode of *Only Fools and Horses* on a big screen TV. As Del Boy came into view, likely engaged in some hilarious money-making scheme, Lucy decided it wasn't worth the risk. She lowered her head and carried on.

She could hear the music from Melanie's open windows long before the house came into view. At some point a neighbour would complain, but Melanie always pushed the boat as far as possible before it happened. Plus, she always invited everyone on the street just to soften them up, aware that as most of them were retired none would show up anyway.

Lucy often wished she had her older boss's outgoing nature, and had often wondered what had pushed Melanie's husband to want a divorce. Finally, after a few drinks in the pub one night, Melanie had confessed that her husband had been a closet homosexual, and had left her for a librarian in the Bristol Central Library. She had since seen them, she had told Lucy, playing frisbee in the park, and had once got drunk enough to call them out for a late night drink. That they were so clearly in love had softened the blow, but only made Melanie more determined to rage against the dying of her own light and create as much havoc as possible while she could still endure the hangovers.

As Lucy reached the steps leading up to the house, she found Melanie standing outside, wearing a slightly resized Elsa-from-*Frozen* dress. Her boss waved a drink at Lucy and shouted over her shoulder for someone inside the hall to pour another and bring it out. They hugged, and Melanie gave Lucy a drunken pat on the cheek.

'We're still waiting for the influx,' she said. 'So far

it's just me and Max from the hobby store, but we're expecting an absolute flood of guests to show up at any moment.'

Max, at least sixty years old and still wearing the tweed jacket he always wore when selling Airfix model kits and fishing supplies, appeared with a drink. He handed it to Lucy, held up his own bottle of Newcastle Brown, and offered a toast.

'To Jesus Christ!' he said, grinning as Melanie rolled her eyes. 'The god of holidays and presents.'

The three of them retired to the downstairs living room, where Melanie did her best to stop Max talking about how virtual model kit apps were gradually stealing his business share. Reginald, not yet banished to the safety of the garden, nestled over Max's knees and looked happy to stay there all night.

'So, did you invite the horse guy again this year?' Max said.

Melanie shrugged. 'I think that postcard might have got lost in the mail—'

The doorbell rang, startling them. Melanie jumped up and bounded out into the hall, returning a moment later trailed by five women from the Tesco Metro up the street. Three of them wore Santa Claus costumes, one was still dressed in uniform, and the fifth hugged a twenty-four-box of own-brand lager against a Disney t-shirt.

'Rocking,' Max said. 'Seven to one. Unless you count old Reg here, then it's down to three-point-five.'

'How many has he had?' asked Angelique, the salty-faced staff manager of the Metro.

Melanie shrugged. 'Not as many as he'd like, I bet.' She lifted her drink. 'Well, Merry Christmas!'

~

A couple of hours later, the party had filled up a little, but with most of the street's younger workers choosing instead to head to the bars in town, the party consisted mostly of middle-aged women, something which left Max delighted. At midnight a handful of drunk students showed up, having heard the sound of a party from the street. Melanie, much to Lucy's horror, quickly disappeared upstairs with one, only for the student to reappear a couple of minutes later to say Melanie was being sick on her bed.

By one a.m., almost everyone had gone. Only old Max was still there, snoring on a sofa with Reginald lying on top of his face. Melanie had recovered enough to nurse down a cup of tea, and Lucy, happy now most people were gone or intoxicated, was playing catch-up with a large glass of the nearly-untouched punch.

'It was a good party, wasn't it?' Melanie slurred, leaning on Lucy's shoulder.

'Nearly the best,' Lucy said. 'Only beaten by the year of the horse.'

'Unbeatable, that one,' Melanie said, then immediately began to cry.

'What's the matter?'

'My children didn't call me. It's Christmas, and my children didn't call.'

'It's December the seventeenth. Most people still have a couple of days of work.'

'It's close enough,' Melanie wailed. She looked about to say something else when a sudden pop like a deflating balloon came from across the room. Reginald's back leg kicked up, then he settled down again. Max grunted, half rolled over, then started to snore.

'Oh dear,' Melanie said. 'That dog's been eating too many sausages. He just guffed on Max.'

For some reason, Lucy found this to be the funniest thing in the world. Before she could stop herself, the rasping siren had come from nowhere, the he-yahs of a donkey on a rusty metal treadmill, hooves scraping as it gasped in great hideous groans.

She slapped a hand over her mouth, but it was too late. Melanie stared at her with eyes wide with shock.

'Good God, is that what it sounds like?'

Lucy wanted the ground to swallow her up. 'Sorry. I suppose you can understand now why I'm so serious.'

Melanie slapped the arm of the chair. 'That has to be the best laugh ever, but I can see why it might put people off.'

Lucy's cheeks were burning. She downed the rest of her punch, then leaned forward and scooped another glassful out of the bowl on the coffee table.

'Four different guys, none of whom knew each other, have given it as their specific reason for dumping me,' Lucy said, a tear springing to her eye as she gulped down another mouthful of punch, then immediately began to sneeze as the Christmas spice which had congealed on the top got sucked into her nose.

'I suppose they didn't get to see your real personality,' Melanie said. 'Just don't make you laugh, right?'

'That's what my dad used to tell them when I brought them home for dinner,' she said. 'They always thought it was a joke and would spend the rest of the evening trying. I used to hate it because boys thought I was pretty and were always asking me out. If I'd been a troll it wouldn't have mattered because everyone would have left me alone.'

'Could be worse. Your husband could be gay.'

Lucy started to laugh but caught herself at the last moment. 'I suppose it could.'

'Gay and very happy. Oh God, my life sucks. Come on, let's drown ourselves in the punch.'

Melanie leaned forward. Before Lucy could stop her, she plunged her head into the punch bowl. Orange-red liquid sloshed onto the floor. Melanie came up with a piece of melon sticking out of one ear.

'It's cold,' she said.

On the other sofa, Reginald guffed again, and this time Lucy didn't bother trying to stop herself laughing, even though she was aware that nearby, dogs were starting to bark with distress, and birds were falling from the sky.

5

ROAD TRIP

SOME MANIAC WAS RINGING THE DOORBELL. LUCY hauled herself up out of bed. She lurched zombie-like for the bedroom door, striking her forehead on the frame as she missed the opening by a couple of inches.

'Hang on, I'm coming!' she shouted, her voice gravelly from the goodbye cigar Melanie had wanted to share, her stomach churning from the kebab she had eaten on the way home. It didn't matter that from her third floor flat the only person who would hear was the grumpy old man who lived downstairs. As the bell rang again, Lucy thought about just pulling it off the wall and going back to sleep, but the visitor might be someone important. She doubted it, but it might. Perhaps someone had seen her vomiting in the street and thought she was the most beautiful woman in the world. He could be standing outside with a huge bunch of flowers, already on one knee, ready to propose.

She leaned against the front door as she pressed the intercom. 'What?'

'Frances? Is that you? How long are you going to keep us waiting?'

'*Dad?*'

'Who else were you expecting at this ungodly hour? Are you ready to go?'

Twenty minutes later, trying to both sober and clean up under a roaring hot shower while her parents drank tea in her small, embarrassingly untidy kitchen, Lucy silently promised to leave her phone at home next time she went out drinking. Of all the people to drunk-text, why had she chosen her dad?

Obviously guilt had made her do it, and at the time it had probably seemed like a good idea.

Hi, Dad, it's me. If you and mum are going down to Cornwall for Christmas, I'd love to come xxxx

She had passed out before reading his answer.

Hello, dear. That would be lovely. We'll pick you up on our way through at about nine.

Eight-fifteen wasn't nine, but that was the least of Lucy's worries. That she had messaged her dad at two-thirty a.m. was bad enough. That she had put four Xs, at least two more than was appropriate to send to a parent, was even worse. Luckily, her dad, Alan, a carpet salesman, wasn't too up to date with the workings and rules of modern social contact.

A rap sounded on the bathroom door. 'Lucy, shouldn't you be out of there by now?' came her mother's voice. 'After fifteen minutes, the water is no longer benefiting your body with its warming effects and is starting to dry your skin out. Do you want to look like a prune by the time you're fifty?'

Lucy groaned. Her mother, Valerie, a lab technician, always had a tidbit of knowledge for something. It was going to be a long journey.

'Are you sure you're not going to be sick in the back?' Alan asked as he pulled the car out of the narrow roadside space on Gloucester Road and jerked it into traffic. 'You can sit in the front if you like.'

'Take this bag, just in case,' Valerie said, passing a plastic bag over her shoulder. Lucy opened it up, catching an immediate whiff of delicatessen products which made her feel even worse than before. She wished she could just rest her head and sleep, but with her father's driving, that was impossible.

'Oh, you ignorant sod,' Alan growled, punching the wheel and hitting the brakes. 'Did you see that, Val? He just cut out in front of me.'

'You had at least five car lengths, dear,' Valerie said.

'But he didn't even indicate.'

Lucy glanced back over her shoulder. The front

door to her flat was still in view. She could still make it if she broke and ran right now, perhaps to barricade herself inside her flat until Christmas was over. She even started reaching for the door handle, but then, with a resigned sigh, remembered her father still had child-locks on his ancient Ford, having never gotten around to taking them off.

~

Taunton Deane Services was an oasis in the desert of poor driving. Lucy headed straight for the toilets, then to McDonald's on the way back, while her father went to get a newspaper and her mother engrossed herself in the journals in the newsagent window.

Three burgers in, Lucy was starting to feel slightly better, when to her horror she saw her father approaching the car wearing a bright red Christmas hat, a fluffy white bobble bouncing about in the wind. As he crossed the road to reach them, a group of lads in a souped-up Subaru gave him a loud blast of the horn then a cheer through open windows. He turned to wave as someone shouted, 'Don't forget to fill me stocking, Grandad! I want the new Chelsea kit and a packet of After Eights for me mum!'

Lucy cowered behind her parents' car in utter humiliation. Her mother, nudging up her spectacles as she walked, arrived with an armful of magazines, lifted an eyebrow at Lucy and then climbed into the car. Alan was still waving at the lads in the Subaru, now parked at the bus station, so Lucy called out to him before getting in behind her mother.

'I can't believe they didn't have *New Scientist*,' Valerie said, arranging the magazines in a fan on her map. 'I mean, I managed to get a copy of last month's *National Geographic*, because they obviously don't check their displays very well, but I'm not sure how I'm going to last the full holiday. What is this country about? Do they think intelligent people only travel by train?'

'Won't there be newsagents in Cornwall?'

Valerie gave Lucy a look in the mirror that suggested the question was farcical. 'It's Christmas, dear. They won't be open. And even if they are, do you think I'll get anything other than *Country Bumpkin Life* or *Tractors Weekly*?'

'Doesn't sound like you're all that keen on this holiday.'

Valerie sighed. 'It was your father's idea. I'm sure it'll be lovely. They're supposed to be turning the place into a Cornish Christmas village. Your father's company is sponsoring the main event, so he's a guest speaker. It's all paid for and everything.'

Lucy couldn't imagine her father doing a speech at anything, but there were more important questions to ask.

'Where exactly are we going, anyway?'

'Oh, didn't we tell you?'

'You were too busy road-raging the entire M5, and I was too busy not being sick.'

'Well, if you will drink too much—'

27

'All right, Mum. I'm sure you were young once.'

'Never,' Valerie said. 'I was born aged fifty, and there I've stayed.' In the mirror, Lucy caught the barest hint of a smile. 'Where's your father gone now?'

Lucy looked out of the window to see Alan heading back into the services' main building.

'Perhaps his stomach's playing up. The doctor put him on a low-carb diet to shift a bit of that weight, but it gives him terrible gas. So … how's work?'

Lucy, still hoping the ground would swallow her, stumbled through some awkward shop talk with her mother until her father reappeared. Alan climbed into the car brandishing a plastic bag. He pulled out a packet of mince pies and held them up.

'Two-for-one offer,' he said. 'Time to get into the spirt of things. Who wants one?'

Lucy, who had finished her fourth burger yet still found her hangover crying out for sustenance, nodded. 'Go on then.'

Valerie shook her head. 'You know what sugar does to me. I'll break out,' she said. 'And you shouldn't either. Remember what the doctor said?'

'Ah, it's Christmas. And I can't let Frances eat the whole packet. It's a nightmare shifting weight at her age, and if she gets too loaded we'll never marry her off. She's only got a few decent years left as it is.'

'How's the carpet trade, Dad?'

'Oh, great, love. I'll tell you all about it over a glass of sherry later.'

'The doctor told you to stay off the booze too,

28

dear,' Valerie said absently, already engrossed in a copy of *History of Britain*.

'Come on, love, it's—'

'Chrisssssmasssss!' Lucy screamed on a sudden whim, channeling her best Noddy Holder. Valerie turned in the seat to frown at her, but Alan just jumped in with a badly hummed bassline, and by the time they turned back on to the M5, they were joyfully slaughtering the Christmas classic to Valerie's obvious distaste.

'So, where are we going again, Dad?' Lucy asked, as Alan blasted the horn at a bus gently pulling out into the middle lane.

'Tintagel,' he said.

'Where's that?'

'Cornwall.'

'I gathered that much, but can't you give me a little more to go on?'

'Just wait,' Alan said. 'You'll see.'

6

BREAKDOWN

'YOU PROMISED ME YOU'D GOT IT DONE,' VALERIE moaned as Alan lifted his phone above his head in another desperate attempt to get a signal. They had somehow managed to break down in the only mobile blackspot along the whole A30. 'I told you it was catching, and you said you'd take it in.'

Alan rolled his eyes. 'Do we have to go through this now?'

'I told you that the gearbox was playing up, and you said you'd get it looked at.'

'I was waiting for the sales,' Alan moaned. 'January's always cheaper.'

'Well, we're screwed now, aren't we?'

'Don't worry, I'm covered. I'll have them out before you can say "Christmas cake".'

'Christmas cake!' Lucy screamed, wondering if she was going insane. At least the freezing cold wind had cleared her hangover, even if the constant roar of traffic was trying to bring it back. She turned, eyes widening as a breakdown truck roared past.

'Wrong company,' Alan said. 'But it was close. Try it again.'

Lucy opened her mouth, but her mother put up a hand. 'Just walk up to the emergency telephone,' Valerie said. 'There's one just up the hill.'

'I'll get run down,' Alan said. 'There's not a single car sticking to the speed limit, the scoundrels. Ah, come on, I've nearly got it. Hello? *Hello?*'

'I'll wait in the car,' Valerie said, crossing her arms, then uncrossing them again to pull open the door and climb in.

Lucy wandered up and down the hard shoulder while her father, finally getting a signal, talked to breakdown services while still wearing his Christmas hat. Lucy was wondering if it was possible to feel even more embarrassed when the Subaru they had seen at Taunton Deane Services, evidently having stopped somewhere on the way, came roaring down the hill. It jerked as it slowed suddenly, then a window wound down and someone shouted, 'Give us a smile, love!' Lucy caught a glimpse of a camera, then the car was past her and gone. She wondered how long it would be before she found herself circulating as an internet meme.

Alan came huffing over. 'All done,' he said. 'They'll be here in an hour.' Then, with a shrug, he added, 'Or two. They said it's busy at this time of year. On the bright side, it's free if they're not here

31

within ninety minutes. So let's hold out for that, shall we?'

Lucy grimaced. The thought of sitting in the car with her bickering parents for the next two hours called for desperate measures. Alan was a keen—if poor—hobby artist, and would certainly have brought his drawing pads with him. Lucy opened the boot and found them neatly packed into a satchel tucked alongside her mother's suitcase. Lucy pulled one out, along with a marker pen her father used when cartooning took his fancy, even though he'd barely got beyond stick men.

'Where did you say we were going?'

'Tintagel … hardly the atmosphere for a little watercolour, is it?

Lucy scrawled the village's name down on the pad and jogged to the roadside, holding it up in the air.

'Wishful thinking, love, but you'll never get a lift from here,' Alan said from behind her, nearly shouting to be heard over the roar of the traffic. 'Cars accelerate too hard down the hill; they'll never see your sign in time—'

'Ah-ha!'

To Lucy's astonishment, a small van indicated and pulled in a short way down the hard shoulder. Alan's mouth was so wide he looked like a drowned fish.

The door of the van opened and a young man got out. Lucy immediately felt a little tickle of excitement. He was in his early thirties, good-looking and broad-shouldered. Dark hair with a few blond highlights was neatly cut and he had just the faintest wisp of a beard.

32

'Tintagel or anywhere,' she muttered, taking a few steps forward.

'Do you want a lift?' he called. 'We're going your way.'

Lucy walked a little closer to the van. It was a light brown colour, with a circular design on the back displaying several lumps of brown with spots of colour in an irregular stack. She frowned. Of all the things—

'Valerie!' Alan hollered beside her, making her flinch almost enough to fall into the oncoming traffic. 'Can you come out here, please?' As a bemused Valerie climbed out of the car, Alan pointed at the brown van and the young man standing beside it with one hand on the rear door, one leg crossed over the other.

'What's going on?' Valerie said, tucking a copy of *Scientific American* under her arm.

'Lucy's found an alternative way down to Cornwall,' Alan said.

'Do you want a lift or not?' the young man shouted. 'We haven't got all day. We have deliveries to make.'

'I'm coming!' Lucy called, wondering if perhaps this trip would have some benefits after all. The man was still standing there, a wry but heavenly smile on his face. Even though from the wing mirrors it appeared there were at least two other people in the van, the thought of sitting next to the young man for the next couple of hours had an appeal that Lucy couldn't resist.

'Oh no you're not,' Alan said. 'Not without your mother. I'll stay here and wait for the breakdown crew.'

'Dad, please, I'll be all right.' *I don't need a chaperone,* she wanted to add, but was afraid the young man would overhear.

'I'm not letting you get into that van with a group of fudge packers,' Alan said. Valerie winced. Then, like Lucy had, she noticed the sign.

Bale & Sons, Tintagel, Cornwall
Finest Cornish Fudge Makers
Packaging and Delivery

'I'm not hitch-hiking,' Valerie said. 'What do you think I am?'

'They're going right there,' Lucy said. 'Come on, Mum.' Then, remembering she was over thirty and the van's address made her quite safe, added, 'I'll go on my own if you like. I'll meet you there.'

Valerie shook her head. 'Not a chance. All right, if you insist on this madcap plan, let's go.' She turned to Alan and winked. 'It's Christmas, after all.'

7

HITCHHIKING

'He'll be all right,' Valerie said, sitting beside Lucy in a rear seat. 'He's got his newspaper, and he'll probably take a nap. He's getting too old to drive such distances in one go anyway.' Then, turning to the three men squeezed into the seat in front of them, she added, 'I'm Valerie Scullion-Drake, and this is my daughter, Lucy. Unfortunately I've forgotten your names, so run them past me again. You know the rule of seven, don't you? Well, I pride myself on three. Back at university I was famous for knowing the names of everyone on campus.'

Lucy squirmed with embarrassment, but none of the three men seemed to notice her discomfort.

'Dan,' the handsome young man said, reaching around to shake Valerie's hand, before offering it to Lucy, who gave hers a surreptitious wipe to rid it of sweat before taking his. 'It's a pleasure to make your acquaintance.'

'Mark Bale,' the older man said as he drove, glancing at them in the mirror. 'Bale's Fudge has been in my family for three generations. I'm hoping one of these lads will take over when I'm gone, but I suppose we'll have to see.' He glanced across the seat, frowning for a long time at the young man sitting in the middle.

'Tarquin,' he said, holding out a hand decorated with half a dozen gaudy rings.

'It's really Trevor,' Mark said. 'But he hates it, don't you, Tarq?'

'Like a fox hates the hounds,' Tarquin said.

'Or a farmer hates a prolonged dry spell,' Mark added with a grin.

'That's right, Dad. Cha-ching.' Tarquin spun and gave his father a solid high-five.

Lucy, somewhat overwhelmed by the absurdity of the situation, bellowed a sudden donkey roar before she knew what was happening. She slapped a hand over her mouth and squeezed back into the seat, hoping the shadows would swallow her up.

'My word, what was that?' Dan said, giving her a wide grin. 'Dad, I think you've got a wheel loose.'

Lucy glared at him, her anger tempered only by her own shame. Valerie gave her a pat on the knee and a long, clinical sigh.

'Asthma,' Lucy croaked, at the same time that Valerie said, 'My daughter has a rather unique laugh, I'm afraid. You're not a fan of it, are you, dear?'

'Mum, can you give it a rest?'

Dan laughed, and Mark gave a polite chuckle.

Only Tarquin, who nodded knowingly, seemed to understand.

'So … you're heading for Tintagel?' Mark asked, breaking the growing awkwardness before it could expand like a balloon to fill the entirety of the van's interior. 'You must be part of the Christmas Extravaganza.'

'You know about it?' Valerie asked.

'Oh, yes. Everyone in the village is so excited. No idea how they're going to pull it off in that windy little place. I think they're even hoping for snow. Chance'll be a fine thing. It hasn't snowed at Christmas in 'Tagel in thirty years. They'll probably get the mist, though. That's all you get at this time of year. Mist and wind, and sometimes buckets of freezing cold rain.'

'Sounds inviting,' Valerie said. 'My husband's company is one of the sponsors.'

'Drake's Carpets?' Dan asked.

'That's the one. How did you guess?'

'Your old man had the look of a carpet salesman,' Dan said.

'Is that a dig at my dad?' Lucy snapped, still angry at being called on her laugh. Dan might be handsome, but she was developing a resentment toward him which she knew she would brood over until it turned into open dislike.

Curtains for any holiday romance then, but she knew from experience that as soon as she rolled out the laugh she was just as well to catch the nearest boat out to a rugged, offshore island.

'And that you have a Drake's Carpets banner on

37

your car,' Dan added, lifting an eyebrow which only made her angrier. 'That's the reason Dad slowed. We wondered what the event's sponsor was doing parked up on the hard shoulder.'

'I'm afraid my husband is as poor at car maintenance as he is at dressing,' Valerie said. 'But he has plenty of other qualities.'

'You could get the lad here to take a look at it when we get back,' Mark said. 'He's great under a bonnet.'

'You're a mechanic?' Lucy said, turning to Dan, finding a chance to win back some points. 'How … educated.'

'Lucy, dear, stop flirting,' Valerie said, seemingly without any kind of social awareness as she patted Lucy on the knee and rolled her eyes at Mark. 'And as a travel agent, you're hardly in a position of industrial authority. We did try to get you into university, but you were too busy playing around.'

'I wasn't playing around!' Lucy stammered, aware the situation was going from bad to worse. 'I was travelling.'

'Well, however you like to call it.'

'Actually, it's Tarquin who's the mechanic,' Mark said, to which Tarquin lifted his hands and did some squeezing motions in the air.

Lucy was ready to open the side door and throw herself out on to the A30. Had she been able to guarantee a martyr's death, she would have done, but Mark was driving far too close to the bouncing safety of the grass verge to guarantee a swift and painless death.

'I suppose you're a surfer,' she said, grasping at one last chance to drag herself off the foot of the social Premier League. 'Or what, a builder?'

'I'm a dentist,' Dan said, then made a drilling sound with his teeth and winked.

'Proud of my boys,' Mark said. 'Their dear mother would be, too.'

Lucy decided it was best to just shut up. Valerie frowned as she processed the connotations of the statement, then opened her mouth, perhaps to ask for details on the Bale family history. Tarquin got in their first, holding up a folded paper bag.

'Anyone for fudge?' he asked, looking around. 'I packed some this morning.'

'Christ, you pick your moments, lad,' Mark guffawed, leaning on the wheel. Lucy slapped a hand over her mouth to avoid a sudden expulsion of laughter. Dan grinned. Valerie just nodded humourlessly and held out a hand to receive a crumbly rectangle of light brown fudge.

Lucy was still glaring at Dan when Mark shouted, 'Look at that clown. Didn't indicate or nothing.'

She was vaguely aware that a tractor had just pulled out, then she was jerking forward, hitting her stomach on the seat in front, and the four McDonald's burgers she had eaten just an hour before were redistributing themselves in a dramatic modern art canvas all over Dan's shirt.

8

GLAMPING

'YOU SHOULD HAVE HAD YOUR SEATBELT ON,' Valerie said, waving at the three men as the van pulled away. 'That was desperately embarrassing. Sometimes I think you're thirty going on twelve.'

'I didn't know a tractor was going to pull out.'

'This is Cornwall, Lucy. That's all they do. Pull out, block roads, and drop muck everywhere. Come on, let's go and find our lodgings so we can get our bearings before your whirlwind of a father arrives.'

Lucy had never considered her father to be a whirlwind, but the thought of finding a place to hide away for the next few days, or at least until she could find a way to escape back to Bristol and, ideally, out of the country, was appealing.

'Where is it?'

Valerie held up a piece of paper. 'Mark said this was it. Lansdowne Holiday Villas.'

They were standing on a narrow two-lane road

sparsely populated with residential properties. During the last few minutes of their doomed journey Lucy had caught glimpses of the sea between hills, so had a vague idea that they were on a clifftop plateau. They had passed a primary school a few minutes before, and seen a couple of shops. 'That's the old post office,' Mark had said, pointing to a decrepit old building which looked anything but, 'and King Arthur's Castle is down there. Not really his castle, though,' he added, dampening Lucy's excitement before it had even roused itself off the floor. 'More a marketing gimmick. Nice views, but not much to see unless you like your ruins.'

'Well, it can't be down there, because that's just a farm lane,' Lucy said, pointing to the cracked, weedy tarmac that curved into a valley on the other side of a cattle grid. 'He must have dropped us off in the wrong place.'

'Oh, you're too distrusting,' Valerie said. 'Considering you insulted and then vomited on his son, he was a perfect gentleman. I found them quite charming. Local, but charming.'

'Local? Mum, you're a snob.'

Valerie smiled. 'Oh, look at you, defending them. See, you did like them. You were quite taken with that Dan, weren't you? I'll have to seek out Mark's shop later and ask if he's single. It might be your last chance.'

Lucy's cheeks plumed with heat despite the damp chill in the air. 'You wouldn't—'

'I suppose that would depend on how entertained

this little place can keep me,' Valerie said. 'It might slip my mind.'

Lucy stalked a few paces down the farm lane, wondering whether there would still be local buses this late in the day which could take her to somewhere resembling civilisation. She was about to turn back to pick another argument with her condescending mother when she noticed a sign hidden by grass on top of a gatepost beside the cattle grid.

Welcome to Lansdowne Holiday Villas

'Mum, I've found it.'

Valerie glanced at the farm lane. 'Do you think we ought to call a taxi to take us down there? There could be all sorts of wild animals. What is it they have around here, the Beast of Bodmin?'

'Bodmin's miles away.'

'Feline-type creatures often have a territory ranging in the tens of miles depending on the availability of prey,' Valerie said, holding up a copy of *National Geographic* and slamming it down on her knee like a judge's gavel. 'It says it right here.'

'Well, if it's a man-eater, I'm sure it would find plenty to eat in Bodmin,' Lucy said. 'Unless you were going to make some witty remark about these people not being human?'

Valerie smirked. 'I wouldn't dream of it,' she said. 'Come on, let's go and find our palace.'

❧

'Mum, it's a tent.'

'"Glamping", your father called it. I had no idea what he meant until now.'

'And there I was thinking you knew everything.'

'I'm a scientist, dear. I keep up to date on what matters, not passing fashion trends.'

The owner of Lansdowne Holiday Villas, a woman called Theresa (pronounced, irritatingly, with a 'Th—' sound) who reminded Lucy of a vole with curtains for hair, ducked her head, widened her eyes and shook her head back and forth in the strange way Lucy had come to understand meant she was waiting for a response.

'It's delightful,' Valerie said, amazing Lucy with her ability to refute the intrusion of sarcasm. 'I mean, it's like a holiday villa, but it's a tent.'

Theresa clicked her fingers with an extravagant motion as though asking a band to keep time. 'That's glamping.'

'And these awnings are secured, aren't they?' Valerie asked, tugging on the nearest one. 'I mean, it gets pretty windy around here, doesn't it?'

'They'd survive in a gale,' Theresa said. 'Almost as solid as actual walls.'

'Why don't they just have solid walls? Planning permission?'

'That's glamping,' Theresa said, as though that were the answer to everything. 'It's the current trend. Camping, but with glam.'

'That's glamping,' Lucy repeated, trying to click her fingers, but failing due to the numbing cold. She stared at Theresa, little more than hair and an apron over bone, wondering if years in this hostile climate could acclimatise a person.

'It has all the mod cons of a proper holiday villa,' Theresa continued. 'You've got a cooker and a shower, hot water, heaters in there.'

'But snakes can still get in?' Valerie asked.

'Well, there aren't really any in Cornwall to speak of, and if there were, they'd likely be hibernating.'

'But technically, a snake could enter this tent?'

Theresa shrugged. 'I suppose technically. Would you like me to call a dealer and arrange for one to be brought over to do a test? I'm pretty sure there's one in Camelford.'

From the way Theresa peered up at her mother from behind her spectacles, not a hint of sarcasm or amusement on her face, Lucy felt the onset of another bout of laughter. She slapped a hand over her mouth as the first violent sound popped out.

Valerie jumped and turned to look at her with a frown on her face. 'Oh, dear, will you keep a lid on it?'

Theresa just lifted an eyebrow with exaggerated slowness, as though the wisp of silver hair weighed too much to move in one go.

'I imagine that would scare them off if any did get in,' she said, with no visible signs of mirth. 'Perhaps keep a book of jokes next to your bed just in case.'

'Well, I suppose it will do,' Valerie said, taking the key to a padlock hooked through a metal ring which was all that would protect them from the night's evils. It looked so flimsy Lucy felt certain she could snap it in her fingers. 'It looks quite cozy really.'

'You'll be back next year,' Theresa said. 'They always come back.'

'Isn't that a horror movie?' Lucy muttered under her breath as her mother said, 'Well, should we expect a visit from last year's residents?'

'Weren't open in the winter last year,' Theresa said.

'Well, that's a relief, I think. Come on, Lucy. Let's get settled in before your father arrives. He'll be nervous enough as it is with his upcoming speech.'

'Are you chaps down for the extravaganza?' Theresa said.

'My father's company is the main sponsor,' Lucy said, feeling a rare moment of pride. Much as she belittled her father, he had built up Drake's Carpets from nothing. According to her father—admittedly not the most reliable resource—the company was the ninth biggest carpet retailer in Bristol, which sounded more impressive when he pointed out that the top five were national chain stores, and therefore "in their own separate league but for the ticker tape."

'Is it really?' Theresa nodded. 'Is that why they only have paper cups?'

'You'd have to ask him about that,' Valerie said, visibly bristling. Lucy wondered if her mother could possibly up her vomiting over the local dentist by picking a fight with a local grandmother over paper cups. And all on their first day.

'Come on, Mum,' Lucy said, praying the tent had

Wi-Fi, or at the very least a television. 'Let's not keep Theresa from her work.'

'It's Th-eresa,' the old woman said. 'Back in my teaching days a mistake like that would have got you the switch. Now, be sure to call if you need anything. I'll be over in the farmhouse behind that muck spreader over there. Office hours are until seven; after that you'll have to wait until morning. Oh, and if you could, keep a lid on that laugh at night, young lady. I don't want it scaring any of the other glampers.'

As the old woman hobbled off, Valerie turned to Lucy. 'Well, you heard her. No laughter, no fun. Should we trust your father or demand we leave in the morning?'

Lucy, who until now had considered leaving to be the best of a multitude of options—others including running herself over with the muck spreader, and leaving the tent flaps open in the hope of being eaten by snakes—found herself leaning toward her father's side.

'Well, Dad never does anything without throwing himself into it, does he?' Lucy said. 'I say we give him the benefit of the doubt.'

Valerie smiled. 'All right, dear. Come on, let's find out what delights glamping holds.'

They went inside the tent. Built on a wooden frame with a taut awning pulled over fixed metal poles, it contained proper beds, a dining table, and a central section that had a kitchen sink and cooker on one side and a shower and toilet on the other.

'Could definitely be worse,' Valerie said, opening

the fridge and pulling out a bottle of complimentary local cider. 'I'm warming to it, at least. Metaphorically, I mean. It's still freezing cold in here. We'd better find the thermostat before we freeze to death.'

It was hardly Arctic conditions, but after an afternoon bumping around in a crowded fudge van followed by a long walk down the farm lane, Lucy was ready for an early night. She inspected the showers and toilet, and was relieved to find the water in the tap ran hot. She was in the middle of freshening up when she heard her mother talking to someone on the phone.

When she came back around the tent's front, her mother was just hanging up, rolling her eyes as she did so. She looked up at Lucy and smiled.

'Well, that was your father,' she said. 'Surprise, surprise, he made a mistake. The breakdown truck dropped him off in Bideford, a couple of hours north of here. He decided it was too late to travel down tonight, so he's got himself a hotel and will meet up with us in the morning.'

'Oh.'

Valerie nodded. '*Oh* is about how I would describe it, too. You know it leaves us only one option, doesn't it?'

'Yes?'

Valerie lifted a conspiratorial eyebrow and grinned. 'Pub.'

9

NIGHT OUT

'Look, Mum, I'm perfectly okay with staying in and watching the TV. I mean, look, it actually works. They don't have Sky, but we could watch *Eastenders*, or there are some DVDs here. *Frozen*?'

Valerie, standing by a wardrobe next to the double bed, was shrugging on a business suit. As Lucy watched with horror, her mother produced a fake fur scarf and wrapped it around her shoulders.

'How do I look?'

'Like Cruella de Vil.'

Valerie lifted an eyebrow. 'Would it work better if I wore contacts?'

'It would be worse. Then you would definitely be Cruella de Vil. People would shut away their dogs.'

'Come on, dear. You can't go out for a night on the town dressed in jeans and a T-shirt.'

'Jeans, a T-shirt, and a jumper, actually,' Lucy said, holding up what she intended to wear, if she couldn't talk her mother out of it. 'I get the impression this isn't some party hotspot.'

'What about the Christmas Extravaganza we're supposedly here for?'

'I don't think it's started yet.'

Valerie smiled. 'Well, let's go and start one of our own.'

'Mum, are you sure you don't have a mental illness? Like, I don't remember you going to the pub ever.'

'Of course I have. I used to pick you and your drunk friends up from those dives on Gloucester Road because your father didn't like driving after dark.'

Lucy felt a fresh wave of embarrassment. 'Yeah, I remember that.'

'You never were good in the car after a few drinks. After today I'd suggest you're getting worse.'

Lucy pulled on her jumper. It was a grey monstrosity from Next which Melanie had got her for her birthday "as a laugh", but if it kept her safe from whatever barbarians or Vikings populated this nowhere little village, it would be worth it. Protecting her mother from being dragged off out to sea might prove a little more difficult.

'Oh, you're not going out like that, are you?'

'Mum, just leave it.'

'I know you don't want anyone trying to make you laugh, but you might as well have a sign saying "misery guts" taped to your back.'

'Well, if the car hadn't broken down I'd write one.'

Valerie patted her on the arm. 'Come on, dear. If I can force a sense of enjoyment into myself, then you can. Let's go paint this village red.'

Outside, the holiday park was dark and silent. A couple of lights shone from nearby tents, and Lucy found herself staring fondly at a line of actual villas across the way, even though the tent wasn't as bad as it had looked from the outside.

'Where's the road?' Valerie asked.

'It was over there, I'm sure,' Lucy answered, pointing toward the farmhouse. The muck spreader had thankfully been moved, and a couple of outside lights made it possible to walk across the yard without stepping in any of the cowpats which had been left lying around like giant brown-green stepping stones. As they spotted the lane leading up to the main road, Lucy noticed a downstairs light was on in the farmhouse, the curtains pulled back. Curiosity made her peer through the window, into a quaint cottage kitchen. Theresa clearly enjoyed more home comforts than she provided her guests.

Lucy was about to shrug and move on when the old lady herself suddenly swung into view, wrapped in the arms of a stiff-shouldered man, his hair a strange mess of twigs. As Lucy's jaw dropped, Theresa made an extravagant turn then rolled herself into an awkward spin. The man, arms stiffly pointing out, stared with dead eyes out of the window as he passed.

'A scarecrow,' Valerie whispered, so close that Lucy let out a little gasp of horror. 'She's dancing with a scarecrow. Come on, I think we'd better get up to that main road.'

They hurried along as the lane wound up out of the valley, holding each other by the arm. Lucy was too scared to look through the dark gateways they passed, but Valerie let out occasional bursts of laughter as though this whole experience was nothing more than a theme park attraction.

Lights came into view as they rounded a last bend and found the main road ahead of them. With the street lights spread out it was barely lighter than the farm lane, but at least signs of normal life came from the line of houses opposite. Through a window Lucy saw a family watching TV. In an upstairs window a couple of doors along, a man was putting up a Christmas tree.

'Look, dear, fairy lights!'

Valerie was pointing a few doors up from the farm entrance. As Lucy stepped over the cattle grid and it came into view, she marveled at the Christmas display set up in the front garden. Illuminated snowmen and elves nodded their heads, while on the roof a Father Christmas standing on a sleigh pulled by six reindeer was waving his hand in a hypnotic metronome.

'Isn't it pretty?' Valerie took Lucy's arm and leaned against her shoulder. 'I'm so glad you decided to come, dear,' she said. 'Christmas will be really special this year. At least, once your father finally shows up. I have a really good feeling about this.'

'An hour ago you were looking for local bus stations on the internet.'

Valerie laughed. 'Nothing like a few fairy lights and a glass of G&T to get one into the Christmas spirit,' she said.

'So you have been drinking! I knew it.'

'Only the one. You took so long choosing that awful sweater that I didn't have much choice. There was quite a booze selection in one of the cupboards. I think the previous tenants must have left the bottles behind.'

'I hope that's the only place Theresa forgot to clean.'

'Fingers crossed. Come on, dear. The night is young.'

They walked up the street, past the house laden with Christmas lights. A family with two children and a dog were taking pictures, so Valerie offered to take a group photograph. In exchange, they were informed that the best local pub was another hundred metres along, a short way down a road to the right.

Five minutes later, it came into view. The building looked at least a thousand years old, but through the small windows she saw a cozy interior. A large Christmas tree stood in an alcove next to a roaring fire, while the windows themselves were hung with fairy lights. Over the door, a painted sign identified the pub as The Lighthouse Keeper.

'Are you ready for this?' Valerie said, hurrying ahead and taking hold of the door. With a sudden flourish, she threw the door open and bellowed, 'Merry Christmas!'

Lucy, desperately wanting to flee away into the

night, had no choice but to trail her mother inside and pull the door closed.

'Merry Christmas,' she muttered, feeling her cheeks redden.

'Same, lass,' was the only response, from a thickly bearded man sitting in a corner booth. Beside the bar, an ancient Labrador lifted its head and gave a wheezy bark.

'Where's the party?' Valerie said, seating herself on a stool next to an empty bar.

'I think it fell asleep,' Lucy said, pointing to the bearded man, who was now leaning over the table, snoring quietly, one hand still gripping his pint.

10

THE LIGHTHOUSE KEEPER

THE ONE SAVING GRACE ABOUT DRINKING IN A nearly empty pub was that there were few people for her mother to embarrass her in front of. Valerie, delightfully going through the backline of sherries and ports, insisted on putting all the Christmas songs on the ancient jukebox standing in one corner, even though they had nothing post-1990. The dog, clearly familiar with some of the tunes, let out a series of short barks on each beat of Shakin' Stevens' *Merry Christmas Everyone* then whined right through Wham's *Last Christmas* as though George Michael had been a personal friend.

The landlord, a jovial balding man with cherry red cheeks who had introduced himself as Jeremy "Jed" Penrose, grinned as he set down two glasses containing a clear liquid topped with sparkly coloured flakes.

'On the house. Last year's Christmas spice voddy.

Need to clear it out to make way for this year's brew before the crowds show up next week.' He set one down for himself, then leaned under a row of low-hanging pint jugs on hooks, each with a person's name above written on a sticker, and bellowed, 'Col, lad! You want one?'

The snoring fellow lifted a hand then dropped it again. His snoring barely broke stride.

'Guess that's a no. Right, ladies, Merry Christmas. Down the hatch.'

Lucy glanced behind her, wondering if they were about to get kidnapped, then saw her mother lifting one of the glasses and realised it was a salute to drinking, rather than an invitation to follow Jed into some damp, gloomy smuggler's cellar.

'Santa, Mary, and Joseph,' Jed exclaimed as he set his glass down. 'Gone a little fallow since last year, I think.'

Valerie sniffed as she wiped away a tear. Lucy sneezed. 'Merry Christmas,' she gasped. 'Is the pub always this quiet? It's Friday night, yeah?'

'Kids all gone down Truro,' Jed said. 'Rented mini-bus. Col didn't want to go. Early start in the morn, putting up the stage.'

There was a lot for Lucy to digest even in such a short statement. Paramount was that Col had been referred to as a kid. Then there was something about a stage. And something else about people actually existing in this end-of-the-world village.

'Would that stage have anything to do with the Christmas Extravaganza?' Valerie asked.

'Ah, everything,' Jed answered. 'Setting it up on the cricket ground back up the road there. That's where they're doing the concert. You know who they've got coming in?'

'Surprise us,' Valerie said.

'Slade. With Nod and Jim. Original lineup. One night only, Christmas Eve. Word is they're only going to do the one song then helicopter out. Top secret.'

'I thought they were all dead,' Valerie said.

'Nah, that's the Beatles.'

'But aren't two of them—'

A creak from behind them announced the arrival of a new patron. Dressed in a floral Hawaiian shirt, Tarquin entered, accompanied by two men in overalls.

'All right, lads,' Jed greeted them. 'Pints? Or do you want something poncey, Tarq?'

Tarquin grinned. 'White wine spritzer, poured over ice, from left to right. Only joking. I'll have a Worthy.'

'Good lad. Still waiting for the Christmas wine shipment. Horse and cart broke down.' He turned to wink at Lucy and Valerie, just as Lucy was beginning to feel the closing of another pair of redneck curtains.

'Oh, hello again,' Tarquin said, noticing the women. 'Glad to see you've settled in and found your way to the best pub in town.'

'Best and only pub!' Jed bellowed, running a biro along the back of the hanging pint mugs, making a surprisingly musical sound. 'Well, I suppose you could mention the Cornishman, and the Castle Hotel has a bar ... but we won't worry about that.'

Tarquin and his friends pulled up three stools around the bar. Tarquin introduced the others as Rod and Joe, then gave a quick recap of how they had all met, kindly leaving out the morning's embarrassing incidents.

Valerie excused herself to visit the toilet, leaving Lucy alone with the three men. Rod and Joe seemed pleasant enough, if a bit rough for her liking. She had a growing urge to ask if only gay men were allowed to have more than three letters in their name when Tarquin turned to his friends and said, 'Lucy's father's company is the main sponsor for the Extravaganza.' Turning back to Lucy, he added, 'You have no idea how excited everyone around here is. It's going to be incredible. Preparations kick off bright and early tomorrow morning.'

'You lads get the tractor running?' Jed asked.

'In the end,' Rod said.

'Took a while,' added Joe.

'Carburettor had burst,' Tarquin finished, before beginning a lengthy monologue about the inner workings of a tractor engine which lost Lucy after a couple of sentences. Finally, Tarquin turned on his stool and called, 'All right, Col? Ready for tomorrow?'

The sleeping man flapped a hand.

'He's good to go,' Tarquin said. 'We start at six a.m.,' he told Lucy. 'The stage has to go up, followed by the sound system, the awnings, the seating areas, everything. In the afternoon we have a specialist coordinator coming in to get everything sorted out properly. The day after tomorrow we have all the food stalls arriving, and the German carolers will be coming on Monday. Tuesday everything kicks off. It's going to be crazy. Every guesthouse in North Cornwall is full. By New Year, Tintagel with be known as Cornwall's Christmas Village.' He rubbed his hands together. 'And Dad'll sell a ton of fudge.'

'Thinking about going over B&Q and getting a few more chairs,' Jed said. 'Reckon it's worth it, Tarq?'

'As worth it as a raincoat in April,' Tarquin said, flapping his hands. The others laughed, but Lucy slapped a hand over her mouth. Tarquin noticed and gave a slight frown, but said nothing.

'Um, maid, your old dear's been in the cornhole a while now,' Jed said to Lucy. 'Might be worth giving her a holler.'

Lucy took a few seconds to process and translate the information. Then, with a sudden sense of worry, she stood up. 'I'll be back in a moment,' she said.

Groans came from behind the locked toilet cubicle door. 'Mum?' Lucy called, giving the door a light tap. 'Are you all right in there?'

'Just having a moment,' came Valerie's voice. 'Don't worry about me. I'll be out in a sec.'

'If you're sure.'

'I'm sure, dear.' Valerie gave a little cough and spat something out. Lucy winced, hoping her mother had made it to the bowl in time, then went back into the bar.

A new customer had come into the bar and was sitting behind Tarquin, Joe, and Rod. The woman was about her own age, but taller, slimmer, more attractive, and, judging by her clothes, significantly more wealthy. Lucy's first reaction was one of surprise, that a woman as clearly classy and beautiful as this would be alone in a local's pub in a quiet Cornish village, but her second was the obvious frostiness between her and Tarquin. The woman was staring at the newest model iPhone, while stirring a glass of whisky with a straw. Tarquin, formerly flamboyant, was hunched over his drink, staring into the glass, while behind him Rod and Joe talked quietly about cars.

Lucy sat back down at the bar. The woman looked up, gave her a thin smile, then lifted her drink and downed it in a single swallow.

'I suppose there's not much going on tonight,' she said, standing up. 'I'll see you again, Jeremy. And Trevor, tell Daniel I'll be stopping by tomorrow. I'm so looking forward to seeing him again after all these years.'

She stood up, swirled a jacket that was clearly made of real fur around her shoulders, and walked to the door in a way that wasn't only seductively elegant but looked catwalk learned. Lucy caught both Rod and Joe giving her surreptitious glances as she opened the door and went out. A moment later a car engine started, far too soon for her to have started it herself, then a roar announced its departure. As it faded into the night, Lucy looked at Tarquin.

'Damn meatgrinder,' he said, not looking up.

'Who was that?'

'That was Elizabeth Trevellian.'

Lucy frowned. The name was familiar.

'Went to our school, now works in the fashion industry. Hideous, both inside and out. She's shown up because she knows the press will be here, and as the most famous person out of Tintagel since King Arthur she'll want her name associated with the event.' Tarquin actually shivered. 'And she'll be hunting my brother. They used to be a couple, until she broke his heart.'

'She broke his heart?'

Tarquin grimaced. 'And his leg. And his collarbone. A long story.'

11

CELEBRITY

'Do you think Theresa will have any paracetamol?' Valerie asked, rubbing her head.

'I could go and ask. If not, there might be a shop open. I'm sure we passed a general store last night.'

Valerie grimaced. 'Could you, dear? I'll sit here and vegetate in front of the television, if that's all right by you.'

Lucy couldn't help but smile. Aware she had to keep an eye on her mother, she had taken it easy on the drink last night, and now found her mother's discomfort of great amusement. 'Hot chocolates tonight, hey?'

Valerie forced a smile. 'Sounds perfect. And an early night.'

Lucy left her mother to her hangover and headed out. No one answered when she knocked on Theresa's door, so she headed straight up the lane to the high street. In daylight, with a bright sun shining overhead, the wilds of Cornwall were a lot more pleasant. Rolling hills dipped into a forested valley, and in the distance rose the first grey-green mounds of Bodmin Moor. And, as she crested the hill and turned onto the high street, she caught sight of the Atlantic beyond the cliff at the end of the gently sloping road. Breakers rolled in, and on the horizon, the outline of an oil tanker moved slowly from south to north.

She turned left, the same way they had gone the night before. On the opposite side of the street, the decorated house looked a lot different with its lights off, the intricate shapes in the front garden, fitted to the walls, and on the roof difficult to differentiate without colour. The general store she had thought she had seen turned out to be a travel agent, but a little farther on she passed the turning to The Lighthouse Keeper and saw Jed's pub had a signboard outside which said CLOSED.

Not far beyond that, she came to an area of tourist shops and cafés, although most were still closed or just opening up. King Arthur and Cream Teas seemed to be the main themes, but a couple of others sold specialist local art, Cornish pewter products, and handmade trinkets. Bale's Fudge was on the coastal side of the road, like most of the others thankfully closed as Lucy hurried past, afraid of being seen by Dan through the windows. Finally, at the end of the street where her road intersected with two others— one heading inland, a second down a steep hill to Tintagel Castle, and a third out to the large block of the Castle Hotel perched on a headland—she found a Spar that was already open.

She picked up what she needed to revive her hungover mother, but instead of heading straight back, she decided to take a look around. Down a side street off a small roundabout a little way back up the high street she found more tourist shops and a small museum focusing on the King Arthur legend, then the buildings began to thin out. She walked until she was presented with fields sloping away into the valley. She didn't fancy the return uphill journey, so she turned back and instead walked down the road and turned onto the Castle Hotel turning at the end. Perched on a dramatic headland with a view over the ruins of Tintagel Castle, the Castle Hotel was a blocky rectangle complete with fake battlements. A car park sat out front and a modern glass conservatory was tacked on to one side. Through the windows Lucy could see guests eating a buffet breakfast.

Behind it, a gravel lane headed out to meet the South West Coast Path. Lucy hiked up a short way until she found herself presented with a panoramic view of the Atlantic Ocean. Rugged headlands jutted out into the sea as far as she could see in both directions, interspersed by a couple of sandy beaches almost lost into the hazy distance.

She hadn't brought her camera, but she resolved to return again later, perhaps with her parents in tow. Nearby, a coast path sign gave mileages to local beaches and villages. While strenuous cliff hiking hadn't been on her mind when she chose to come to

Cornwall with her parents, a bit of exercise would certainly do her father some good.

With one last look at the spectacular coastal view, she turned and headed back down to the main road. Her thoughts were elsewhere, on previous holidays and possible future ones—a solo trip along the entire coast path might keep her out of society for six blissful weeks or so—when a voice that sounded familiar came shrieking over the light rustle of the wind.

'Get the other angle, Shawn! We've got stately, now we need this one to be windswept. I'll need both for Instagram.'

Lucy paused at a gateway across the road from the Castle Hotel, leaning into the gatepost to allow a protruding hawthorn bush to partially obscure her as she watched the events underway in the hotel's car park.

Elizabeth Trevellian was draping herself over an expensive silver Bentley while two men attempted to photograph her. One was holding a curved reflective screen to capture the light, while the other was kneeling, holding a camera to his eye.

'How does it look?' Elizabeth said. 'Do I look "Cathy" enough?'

The two men exchanged a look. 'It's not bad,' one said.

'Let's try across the street. Get a couple of clifftop shots from that gateway over there.'

Before Lucy knew what was happening, Elizabeth Trevellian and her two companions were walking straight toward her. She could do nothing other than lean on the gate and pretend she was enjoying the view of an empty field.

'Excuse me?' came a voice from behind her. 'Would you mind moving along a little way? We'd like to take a couple of photographs here if you don't mind.'

Lucy turned, feigning surprise. 'Oh, I'm sorry. Sure.'

She paused for a moment, allowing her eyes to examine Elizabeth more closely. While certainly beautiful with cheekbones and jawlines and a pert nose all in the right places, Elizabeth wore a mask of makeup which up close looked possible to peel off.

'Are you all right?'

Lucy started. 'I'm sorry, I was miles away.'

'Look, it's clear you know who I am. If you'd like me to sign something, it wouldn't be a problem.'

'Oh, well, I don't—'

A hand had appeared out of a glove. Nails as perfectly rounded as a doll's protruded from fingers which looked polished. Caught into the situation, Lucy reached into her coat pocket and pulled out the first thing her fingers closed over.

A McDonald's receipt.

Elizabeth smiled as she took it and turned it over. 'Well, if that's all you have … a pen please, Shawn.' She stretched out her other hand without looking down. The photographer rolled his eyes and pulled one from his pocket, placing it gently in Elizabeth's hand with an apologetic look toward Lucy.

'Well, what's your name?' Elizabeth lifted her

eyebrows and leaned forward as though addressing a child. Then, glancing down at the items on the receipt, she added, 'I can tell you have a large family. Would you like it signed to your children, perhaps?'

Lucy felt a sudden sense of epiphany come over her. Smiling, she said, 'Just sign it to Frances Drake.'

Elizabeth started to write, then paused. She looked up and frowned. 'Are you making fun of me?'

Lucy shook her head. 'No. That's my name.' Unable to help herself, she let out a sudden guffaw of grating laughter which made Elizabeth and her crew members take a couple of steps back. 'I don't have my driver's license with me, but if you'd like to come back to my, er, glamp-site, I'd be happy to show you.'

Elizabeth frowned. 'Are you sure you haven't escaped from somewhere?'

'Bristol,' Lucy said.

Elizabeth glanced back at her crew. Shawn shrugged, but the other one hissed, 'It's on the way to London.'

'I know where it is, Peter.' Turning back to Lucy, she said, 'Well, you enjoy the view. I think we'll shoot somewhere else.'

She stuffed the receipt back into Lucy's hand, then waved Shawn and Peter to follow as she headed for the coast path. Lucy watched until they turned out of sight then looked down at the receipt in her hand.

Dear Frank, it said.

With a bemused shrug, Lucy headed back to the campsite, wondering if by now her mother had starved to death, or simply gone back to bed.

12

ONLINE TROUBLES

'I THOUGHT I BROUGHT YOU UP NOT TO BE ENVIOUS of other people,' Valerie said, leaning over Lucy's shoulder and peering at the pictures Lucy was flicking through on her smartphone. 'You should be happy with who you are. You don't need to waste time ogling models on the internet.'

'I'm not ogling. This is that woman we met in the pub last night. Well, I met; you were … um, sleeping in the toilet.'

Valerie gave her a sharp look over the top of her spectacles. 'I was just tired from the journey.'

'Well, anyway, I met her this morning up the street when I went to buy breakfast. Look at that: she has two million followers.'

'Is that a lot?'

'I'd say so.'

'Well, you know that probably only half of those people liked her because they have any interest in her, and half of those people pay any attention to what she posts, and half of those people actually engage with her.'

'Which means she gets something like a quarter of a million likes on each picture she posts.'

Valerie looked at the ceiling, frowning. 'Yes, I suppose so.'

'So she's basically as popular as most movie stars.'

'Ah, it's not real popularity though, is it, all this social media rubbish?' Valerie said.

'I have nine Instagram followers,' Lucy said. 'Two of them are you and dad.'

Valerie grinned. 'I forgot I set up an account. I wondered why they kept sending me emails. I suppose I just wanted to know where you were off to all the time, since you never rang home.'

'I did!'

'Once a month counts as never,' Valerie said.

'Is that a very scientific statistic?'

'No, it's a social one. And aren't they the only important ones these days?'

'Mum, you just said—'

'I was being sarcastic, dear. Listen, after breakfast, why don't we go out for a walk, see if the local museum's open or something? Your father should be here at any time.'

'Sure.' Lucy went to switch off her phone, but suddenly a new picture appeared on Elizabeth Trevellian's Instagram page. It showed the same field gateway Lucy had been watching her from, only now

Elizabeth was draped seductively over the gatepost. The comment underneath read, *"Looking windswept in gorgeous Cornwall this morning! Had to shoo off an enthusiastic local to get this shot—she actually barked at me! Didn't realise speech was still a luxury in this part of the world!"*

Despite having been posted less than a minute previously, the picture had two thousand likes already, and comments were appearing underneath, ranging from commiserations to jokes about the Cornish. Lucy held up the screen for Valerie to see.

'She's talking about me!'

'Oh, dear.' Valerie lifted an eyebrow. 'Did you laugh at her?'

'It's not funny, Mum.'

'Well, a good job it's not. The people in the next tent are still in bed.' At Lucy's frown, Valerie came forward and wrapped her up in a hug. 'Dear, your laugh really isn't that bad. I don't know what the fuss is all about. I'm sure there are far worse laughs in the world. All you have to do is laugh with it, if you know what I mean.'

'You mean enjoy the fact that I can empty a room with it?'

'Well, something like that. Enjoy that people find your laugh entertaining.'

'Most people find it scary. I've almost caused car accidents.'

'You're overreacting.'

Lucy remembered the time she had brayed at a sudden joke while an ex was driving, causing him to swerve and take the wing mirror off a passing car. The next day he had broken up with her.

'No, I'm not.'

Valerie patted Lucy on the arm, then looked up at the sound of a car engine from outside. The vehicle pulled up and came to a stop.

'Oh, that'll be your father. Let's go berate him for going out drinking on his own, shall we? That will cheer us both up.'

Lucy sighed. 'And people tell me I'm unique.'

The car was apparently back in working order. Alan, looking a bit red in the face after what he had claimed was "a pint or perhaps two to get me off to sleep", was pleased to see they had settled in, marvelling at the tent as though it was the best thing in the world.

'And snakes probably can't get in,' Lucy said, finishing the guided tour. 'Although we haven't actually tested.'

'Looks like a palace,' Alan said. 'What's the village like? I had some flyboy on my bum coming up here so I didn't get much time to get a look at it.'

'Quiet,' Lucy said. 'I think Mum raised all the hell there was to be found in the pub last night.'

'You went to the pub without me?' Alan rolled his eyes. 'Shameful.'

'That's what happens when you let me off the leash,' Valerie said with a grim smile. 'For what it's worth I'm glad my protector is back. Lucy's not the best at piggybacks.'

'Don't worry, Dad. I think there'll be plenty more chances,' Lucy said. 'There's not a lot else going on.'

Alan smiled. 'Not yet, there isn't. Everything's about to kick off.'

They secured the tent and headed up to the high street. Alan insisted on greeting everyone they passed and introducing themselves wherever possible, much to Lucy's embarrassment and Valerie's frustration.

The King Arthur museum had just come in sight up ahead when Alan stopped abruptly, causing Lucy to bump into him.

'Oh, there's that chap who gave you a lift yesterday,' he said, pointing at the fudge shop on their right. 'Let's go say hello.'

Before Lucy could stop him, he had marched up to Mark Bale, who was standing outside the fudge shop, writing daily specials up on a chalkboard.

'Alan Drake,' he said, stretching out a hand as Mark looked up. 'You kindly rescued my girls yesterday. Thanks for not abducting them and selling them overseas.'

Mark looked pained as he joined in with Alan's raucous laugh. 'It was no problem at all. I'm glad your car got fixed up all right.'

'As good as it was the day I bought it secondhand,' Alan said. 'Thanks again for giving Valerie and Frances a ride down.'

'Frances?' came a voice from behind them. Lucy gritted her teeth as she turned to find Dan standing in the shop doorway, holding a stack of plastic crates. He was wearing a vest, the defined muscles of his shoulders and arms catching the sun.

'Oh, hello,' she said. 'I, um, would like to apologise about yesterday. Being sick on you and all that.'

'You puked on him?' Alan said. 'Frances, I wonder about you sometimes.'

'Dear, you know she prefers Lucy….'

'Don't worry,' Dan said. 'You can owe me a favour.'

'Sure.'

With a grin he added, 'If I see a Spanish fleet off Tintagel Head up there, I'll give you a call.'

13

THE COORDINATOR

'I think he likes you,' Valerie said. 'I mean, he made a joke at your expense, but he was smiling. That's a good sign.'

'And lucky you didn't laugh at it,' Alan added, stuffing a huge piece of scone into his mouth. Alan, who claimed to have forgotten breakfast, had insisted they stop in a pretty café for a mid-morning cream tea.

'He's already heard her laugh,' Valerie said. 'You let one slip, didn't you, dear?'

Lucy glowered into her hot chocolate as Alan said, 'And they didn't drop you off at the next services? Must be true love.'

'You know we're only joking,' Valerie said. 'Your laugh's not that bad.' She patted Lucy's hand. Lucy said nothing. The photograph Elizabeth Trevellian had posted now had twenty thousand likes. The last time she had checked—during a pretend toilet break

—more than a hundred people had asked for the identity of the "barker" to be revealed in order that they could cross the street should they encounter her. If Elizabeth had caught Lucy's name, life—online at least—could become a complete nightmare.

'You're welcome to each other,' she muttered under her breath while Valerie was trying to dissuade Alan from ordering an extra scone, yet even as she said it, she wondered why it made her feel so catty to have met both Elizabeth and Dan within a few hours of each other. So what if they used to be a couple? Dan was a pig and Elizabeth was a troll. A perfect match.

'Look, we can walk it off by taking the cliff path back around to the cricket ground,' Alan was saying, patting Valerie's hand as though trying to calm an excitable dog. 'I need to keep my strength up. Plus, it's cold, so you lose a lot of body heat that way….'

'In two sweaters your body heat loss will be minimal,' Valerie said. 'Come on, they'll have some food there too. If you eat too much now you won't have any room left.'

Finally persuaded not to order any more, Alan agreed to leave. After a short walk around the King Arthur museum—where displays inside confirmed that the legend had no provable historical link to the village whatsoever—they walked to the end of the street and up to the coast path. Lucy was pleased to see that Elizabeth's Bentley was no longer parked in the car park outside the Castle Hotel. Hopefully she'd already left.

'Look at these views!' Alan exclaimed, as soon as they reached the clifftop. 'You couldn't pay for them, could you?'

'Well, you could if you were willing to move out of Bristol—'

'Let's get a picture,' he said, pulling out his camera and immediately dropping it into a spiny gorse bush by the side of the path. Valerie laughed while Lucy rolled her eyes. Alan grimaced as he pulled his sleeve over his hand and reached in through the spines to retrieve it. 'Right, let's try again,' he said, standing up. 'We can all get in it together.'

The result of much arm stretching and fidgeting was an awkwardly angled shot with half of Lucy's face and the crown of Alan's head missing. In the middle, Valerie's spectacles were so covered in spray that her eyes were obscured, and the only sign they were in Cornwall was a triangle of clifftop in one corner. Alan, however, seemed delighted.

'We'll get that up on the website,' he said.

The cliff walk was a lot more strenuous than the high street, but they came to a sign pointing inland to the cricket ground just before the path dipped sharply into a rocky valley.

'We'll save that stretch for when we need to walk off Christmas dinner,' Alan said.

'Only if the coastguard helicopter's about,' Valerie said. 'If you go down there, you'll never get back up.'

Alan patted his protruding stomach. 'I've barely aged in thirty years. I've forgotten how many features I've turned down for *Men's Health*.'

'So have we,' Valerie said. 'Come on, let's go and find out just what it is you've sponsored.'

They took the path leading back inland, and after a few minutes emerged at a wide cricket pitch sitting prettily on a flattened hilltop with views of the sea to the north and Bodmin Moor to the southeast. Fields surrounded it on three sides, with the first houses of Tintagel's small suburbs on the other. A single-storey pavilion stood at one end of the pitch, but where the cut strip would have been in the middle was now a stage in the process of being assembled.

Several tractors pulled loaded trailers back and forth, and a couple of dozen people were milling around, setting up various stalls and tents. As they approached the pavilion, the sound of *Jingle Bells* came from a speaker hanging from a pole overhead.

'Ah, Christmas,' Alan said. 'The best time of the year.'

'The worst if you're single,' Lucy muttered.

'Not if you're with your family,' Valerie said, putting an arm around Lucy's shoulders and giving her a squeeze.

Lucy closed her eyes for a moment, imagining a deserted beach in Sicily. No one around, just her and a handful of paperbacks, a sea that wasn't yet too cold to swim in, and a little pizzeria just back from the foreshore, with a single unoccupied table outside.

They were still standing around watching developments when a short middle-aged lady wearing a Christmas hat and a string of flashing Christmas lights around her neck appeared out of the pavilion and came hurrying over.

'I thought I recognised you,' she said. 'Alan Drake, isn't it?'

'That's me. And this is my wife, Valerie, and daughter Frances.'

'But call me Lucy,' Lucy said.

'Lovely to meet all of you. My name's Ellie, and I'm the independent coordinator for the Christmas Extravaganza. I run a Christmas holiday village in Scotland, and I'm certain we can capture all the delights of Christmas even down here on the misty Cornish coast. As the official sponsor, you have a couple of things to do, so if you'd like to follow me, we'll take a look at the itinerary over some hot chocolate specials.'

'Hot chocolate specials?' Alan asked, as Valerie looked at him with a familiar raised eyebrow.

'Hot chocolate with marshmallows, clotted cream, and a flake,' Ellie said. Then, clapping her hands together, she added, 'And a dash of Christmas spice. Merry Christmas!'

14

HEART TO HEART

ALAN STAYED WITH ELLIE TO GO OVER THE
Extravaganza's details, with Valerie insisting on
staying too to "protect him from temptation", after it
emerged that Ellie had a veritable cauldron of hot
chocolate brewing over a temporary stove set up
inside the pavilion. 'Enough,' she said, 'for everyone
on site to have at least two cups, because it's a bit
chilly out there.'

With nothing to do but wait around, and already
feeling a couple of pounds heavier than she had been
when she left Bristol, Lucy left her parents to their hot
chocolates and discussions and took a walk around the
perimeter of the cricket ground. From a distance,
everything looked little different from a construction
site she might have seen in Bristol, except for one
small thing.

Everyone involved was wearing a Christmas hat.

Lucy smiled. A man operating a JCB as he

shouted at someone carrying a stack of scaffolding poles while both wore cherry red Christmas hats suddenly seemed like the funniest thing in the world. Lucy felt the urge to laugh but thought better of it.

She had laughed enough on this trip already.

The elation the hats had brought slid like a loose rock into the sea as a new wave of self-loathing took its place. She sat down on a nearby bench, feeling like the world was caving in around her. She could be alone in Sicily right now—*should* be alone in Sicily. Ordinarily she made a token visit to her parents' place on Christmas Day, but had she known they were going to Cornwall she would have had a good excuse not to bother.

'Hey, you over there … why the long face?'

Lucy jumped up off the seat and turned around. Tarquin stood up out of the hedgerow set back from the cricket field's boundary, making Lucy gasp. Wearing a purple satin shirt over faded blue overalls stained with grease, and with a Christmas hat perched on his head, he looked like some kind of cross-dressing goblin caught in the wrong fairytale. With a cheeky grin he picked a piece of bramble off his leg and tossed it back into the grass.

'What on earth are you doing?' Lucy asked. 'I'd like to think you were spying on me, but I've only just sat down, and really, I don't know anyone less likely to be spied on.'

Tarquin held up an armful of fairy lights. 'I'm making a complete circuit,' he said. 'Ellie's instructions. Who in the world makes industrial-grade

79

fairy lights like these? If I could find a supplier, I'd decorate my bedroom.'

Lucy smiled. 'Do you want some help?'

'That would be more than grand. It would be a million.'

'Um, okay.' Feeling an immediate calmness in the presence of the odd mechanic, Lucy waded into the long grass until she was standing at the foot of the bordering hedgerow.

'The trouble I'm having is dragging these along with me,' Tarquin said. 'It would be such a delight if you could carry the reel while I feed them out. Ellie wanted me to make little loops. While aesthetically I'm right with her, physically it's a struggle.'

'I thought you were a mechanic?'

Tarquin gave a high-pitched laugh that was almost as unique as her own. Instead of a rumbling, grating bellow which could crack concrete, however, his had a certain charming appeal.

'Fine tuning, darling. I have Rod and Joe to do all the heavy lifting. I just make the engines purr.' With that he made a drawn out purring sound, followed by a couple of mock cat scratches.

Lucy helped Tarquin haul the reel of fairy lights down out of the hedge. As he arranged them, she pulled it along. Despite his claim, she knew he was hiding muscle behind his campiness because she was exhausted after a couple of minutes. Thankfully, once they were out of the far corner, the hedgerow reverted into a stone wall with a polite grassy top, making progress much faster.

'Are you settling in all right?' Tarquin asked, as they neared the third corner and after it the home straight back to the pavilion.

'Yeah, I suppose,' Lucy said. 'My dad showed up, and my mum has got over her hangover. Tintagel seems a nice enough place.'

'It's okay when you get used to it,' Tarquin said. 'The people are friendly once you get to know them. Very down-to-earth, and a lot more tolerant than you might expect, if you know what I mean.' At this, he gave her a dramatic wink. Then, his smile dropping, he added, 'Most of the undesirables who think they're too big for this place tend to leave as soon as they can. And, if we're lucky, they don't come back.'

'Like Elizabeth Trevellian?'

Tarquin laughed. 'You're an astute one, aren't you?'

'I ran into her this morning on the clifftop. I got the impression from her Instagram that she didn't find me much to her liking.'

'Oh, was that you she described as a barking local? Oh my, did you laugh in front of her?'

Lucy nodded. 'My dad once told me I had a laugh which could sink ships. I know he was only joking, but he was kind of right.'

Tarquin grinned. 'It doesn't hurt to have a surprise weapon, does it?'

'It does if it keeps going off at the wrong time and getting you dumped. My parents make light of it, because it's easier for them to trivialise something they can't change. When I was a little I sometimes thought I wasn't good enough, that I wasn't perfect enough, but when they had to go out to bat for me, they always did. I remember we were at Butlins once and this kid and his dad started laughing at me in the swimming pool. My dad threatened to thump him.'

'The kid?'

Lucy smiled and shook her head. 'The dad. I know my parents love me, and my closest friends at school tolerated it, but it's still a nightmare. I've not had a relationship in years and at this point I'm scared to even try.'

Tarquin paused as he went to twist the fairy light wire around a little fir tree planted just inside the wall and turned to look at her. 'Like that, is it?'

'What do you mean?'

'You know, I sensed it straight away. I have such a nose for these things. Trust me, as the only openly gay kid in my school, I pick up on them right away. You think it's ruining your life, don't you?'

'Of course not,' Lucy snapped. 'I just … try never to laugh.'

'Which is understandable. I used to pretend to like wearing black. But now your defenses have been breached by an unfamiliar enemy.'

'What, Christmas?'

'A Christmas holiday with your parents. Where you're no longer in control. Would I be right in saying that you prefer to travel alone?'

'Are you some kind of fortune teller?'

'Like I say, we're kindred spirits. The times might

be a-changing, as they say, but I'm still a social outcast, and so are you.'

'So, how did you deal with it?'

'The kids at school started calling me Tarquin because it was the gayest name they could think of. The problem was that I liked it, so eventually they had no ammunition. People tried to pick on me, but I rolled with everything they threw at me. Believe me, I still get hassled sometimes in bigger places, but in Tintagel most people who know me have accepted me as I am. It rarely went beyond a bit of gentle name-calling anyway, because I have an older brother built like a battleship and my dad owns the best fudge shop in the village, and no one wants to be barred from that. But mostly because I became comfortable in myself and with who I am.'

'So what you're saying is that I should like my laugh?'

Tarquin grinned. 'Darling, that's exactly what I'm saying.' He spread his arms and looked up. 'I think you should laugh at the top of your voice for as long as possible.' He let go with a sudden burst of laughter so loud it made Lucy cringe. 'Now, I think it's time for an afternoon snack, don't you? It's nearly two o'clock and I know Ellie wanted to give us a pep talk.'

He climbed down from the fence and walked over. He held up his little finger and hooked it. 'You come looking for me whenever you need some advice,' he said. 'But it all stays within the circle, okay? Little piggy promise?'

He gave his finger a wiggle. Lucy noticed he'd

drawn a little smiley face on it. With a grin, Lucy hooked her own around it.

'Right, hot chocolate time,' Tarquin said. 'Then, perhaps later, if we have time, we'll have a little chat about Dan.'

15

CALL TO ARMS

'All right, everyone,' Ellie said, holding up her cup. 'Hot chocolates in the air.'

A sea of steaming cups rose in a salute. Not far from Lucy, a marshmallow overflowed, making a sticky roll for freedom, only to be deftly caught in a waiting mouth. The man hurriedly replaced it with another one from a bowl on a nearby table.

'Three ... two ... one ... Merry Christmas!'

Ellie grinned as everyone cheered and took a sip of their hot chocolate. An older man in a suit decorated with Christmas lights appeared beside her, took the microphone and climbed up onto a chair. He gave the microphone a dramatic tap, then cleared his throat.

'Welcome, everyone, and thank you so much for all your hard work so far. Now that the main team is all present, I thought it would be nice to have some introductions. My name, for those of you who don't know it, is Denzil Porthleven. I'm the head of Tintagel Parish Council, and of the committee which decided to hold this Christmas Extravaganza, both to promote our little village and also to give a bit of a kick to the local economy, which tends to struggle at this time of the year. The good news is that every guesthouse and campsite within a ten-mile radius is fully booked right through to New Year. Now all we have to do is pull this off so they'll all want to come back again next year.'

The crowd cheered. Near the front, Lucy spotted her father standing next to Ellie, his cheeks as red as the Christmas hat he wore. Behind him, Valerie was looking on with a bemused smile.

'Firstly, I'd like to give my warmest thanks to our main sponsor for this event, Drake's Carpets of Bristol.' He reached down and grabbed Alan's hand, hoisting it into the air. The crowd cheered. 'Without Alan Drake here, none of this would be possible. Don't forget, a Drake's carpet is not just a carpet, but also a friend.'

Lucy winced. She had always hated her father's cheesy slogan, but as the crowd cheered again, she wondered if perhaps it was more suitable than she realised. After all, while most independent carpet wholesalers in Bristol had been swallowed up by national chain stores over the last few decades, her father's was still going strong. He had a steady stream of regular customers, and even seemed to be gaining new ones.

'And secondly, I'd like to thank Ellie here, for

agreeing to coordinate this event. Ellie's come all the way from Scotland to be with us over the next couple of days, so we're greatly indebted to her for giving up her time. Ellie, if you please….' Denzil stepped down from the chair and helped Ellie up. She took the microphone and smiled.

'Okay, everyone, thank you so much for all your hard work. My job is to show you how to enjoy Christmas properly. Firstly, let's just point out a few basics. Christmas, as we know it, is currently considered a Christian festival. Therefore, you might think it exclusive to people of a certain religion. Not so. Long before Jesus was a twinkle in his mother's eye, people were celebrating the midwinter around this time. Many of the traditions of Christmas that we have today far predate Christianity. And since all religions and cultures work to the same seasons, and most of those religions and cultures enjoyed some kind of winter solstice festival, it's safe to say that regardless of your background, Christmas is a festival that everyone can enjoy.' She frowned. 'I will accept nothing less than total enjoyment, regardless of your personal beliefs. Is that understood?'

The crowd cheered. Ellie nodded and smiled. 'Good. Now, the basics. To fully enjoy Christmas, you have to fully embrace Christmas. You have to become one with it, let its cheesiness into your heart. And the easiest way to do that is to have a hot chocolate by your side at all times during the day, and a nice glass of mulled wine once the sun goes down. Are you following so far?'

'Yeah!' came a series of calls.

'And now, something I'd like to moan about. Do you know what I heard when I arrived this morning?' Ellie paused, theatrically scanning the crowd. 'JCBs. Tractors. People hard at work.' She sighed. 'Do you know what I wanted to hear?' Another dramatic pause. 'Christmas songs. We have speakers being set up outside. I will not accept such a terrible violation again. If I can't see people singing along to Slade, Wham, or Bing Crosby, I will call a mass hot chocolate break and insist everyone sing along to an obscure Christmas song of my choice. Did you know Bryan Adams put out a Christmas single? It's called *Reggae Christmas*. Don't think I won't make you sing it.'

A few murmurs came from the crowd, mixed with some laughter. Lucy noticed a couple of people nearby pull out their smartphones, no doubt to check on YouTube.

'But,' Ellie continued, 'the basics of Christmas remain no matter what you believe in. And those basics are kindness and generosity. And to show you just how easy it is to give something to someone, I'd like you now to turn to the person next to you and give them a compliment about their appearance. Anything at all. Ready … go!'

Lucy turned, then let out a little gasp. Dan stood right beside her, arms folded. He looked just as surprised as she, and his eyes widened. 'I … uh … I like your, um, shoes,' he stammered, pointing at Lucy's grass-stained pumps.

Lucy stared at him. Up close he was nearly a head

taller than her, and broad enough that he could have enveloped her in a bear hug. She stared at him, wanting to say something nice, but all she could remember was how he had mocked her laugh and then she had thrown up all over him.

'I ... I ... I—'

'See how easy that was,' Ellie said into the microphone, cutting the moment off. 'I bet one or two of you have made a whole new friend.' With a wink she added, 'Maybe even a boyfriend or girlfriend.'

Lucy couldn't help but glance toward Dan, but he was no longer there. Instead, he had slipped away through the crowd and was quietly exiting through a side door. As she watched, someone else detached themselves from the crowd to follow:

A woman wearing furs and a petite Russian hat which made her look as though she had just stepped out of a winter fashion catalogue.

Elizabeth Trevellian.

16

REVELATIONS

'Is my little girl moping?'

Alan leaned around the curtain that was Lucy's only privacy and grinned. Lucy, who had been checking Elizabeth Trevellian's Instagram account, slipped her phone under her pillow and rolled over.

'I have a bit of a stomachache,' she said. 'I think it's too much hot chocolate. Go on, you and Mum go out. I'll stay here and look after the tent.'

Alan shook his head. 'Oh no you don't. We're less than a week away from Christmas and I have my whole family together. Let's go and get dinner at one of the little restaurants up on the high street.'

'I really don't feel like it.'

'Come on, Lucy....'

'I'm tired, Dad. It was a long day.'

Alan smiled again. 'But doesn't a day like that just energise you? I don't think I've ever had so much fun while carrying chairs and setting up tents. My voice is

90

almost hoarse from singing so much, and this Christmas hat is starting to chafe.'

'Really, I just need an early night.'

'Come on, Alan, leave her alone,' came Valerie's voice through the shower door as the water cut off. 'A young girl needs her freedom from us old farts.'

'She has her freedom the other eleven months of the year,' Alan moaned.

'She's an independent woman,' Valerie said. 'And at least she's here. She could have been off in Botswana or somewhere.'

'Sicily.'

'Or there. Come on, we'll get some dinner then I'll show you the pub we found. We'll get in a couple of sherries. Is there any of that bacon left, Lucy?'

'A couple of bits.'

Valerie laughed. 'Well, don't stay up too late as we might need you to go on a food run tomorrow morning.'

'Are you sure you won't come?' Alan asked. 'I mean, if your mother can have a good time, anyone can.'

'I think I'm a bit of a hick at heart,' Valerie said. 'Oh arr, me lover!'

Lucy sighed and lay back on her bed as her father finally gave up and dropped the curtain. A few minutes later they went out, zipping the tent door up behind them.

Returning to her phone, Lucy found that Elizabeth Trevellian's photo had now clocked up over fifty thousand views and a couple of thousand comments, most of them mocking the barking local or offering Elizabeth commiserations on what was perceived as a terrible predicament. Luckily, she had since uploaded new photos which were now getting most of the attention, a couple of her looking seductive on the shoreline of a nearby beach, one of a pristinely manicured hand holding a mug of coffee, and another of a plate of fresh fudge.

Lucy frowned. Yes, there in the description was a hint that it could have been Bale's Fudge: *Went to see an old friend today.*

Most of the comments seemed to think the fudge itself was an old friend, and dozens of people had congratulated Elizabeth on jettisoning her "friend" in order to maintain her perfect figure. Lucy, having seen Elizabeth chasing after Dan, knew otherwise.

But what did it matter? Dan was a pig. Of the two brothers, she much preferred Tarquin, even if he was gay. But if he had grown up with a gay brother, perhaps Dan wasn't a pig after all, and they had just got off on the wrong foot.

'I'm not falling for him,' she whispered, afraid that the tenants of the adjacent tent might overhear. 'I barely know him, and even if I was falling for him, what on earth would he see in me with an ex-girlfriend like … her?'

Now that her parents had gone out, she regretted not taking the opportunity to grab something to eat. The fridge held nothing of interest, and the last hot chocolate during a mid-afternoon break felt an age ago. She searched for local pizza places on her phone, but the only one that delivered closed at eight and it was nearly half-past.

She stood up, pulled on her jacket and slipped on her shoes. Tintagel, what she had seen of it, was a decent-sized village, so there had to be somewhere to get fish n' chips or some other kind of takeaway which she could bring back. The alternatives were horrifying. Eating alone in a foreign country made her exotic; here she would simply be Billy-no-mates. And seeking out her parents and gate-crashing their dinner together was even worse.

Up on the high street, she turned right, having explored the village to the left earlier in the morning. While she remembered a few cafés and restaurants, she hadn't noticed any takeaways. To the right, however, she had only gone as far as the cricket ground, so there might be something along the road past that.

The high street was a bit of a wind tunnel, but the winds she had feared that might come in off the sea were yet to make themselves known. She hurried along past several residential cul-de-sacs where most of the houses had Christmas lights in their windows, and a few even had garden displays or lights covering the shrubs and trees. Despite all the emotions plaguing her, Lucy was beginning to feel the spirit of Christmas soaking into her, and she even found a smile as she passed a house with an illuminated Father Christmas dangling theatrically by one hand from an illuminated ladder stretching up a side wall.

She reached the cricket ground, where a huge sign

now stood over the car park, announcing TINTAGEL CHRISTMAS EXTRAVAGANZA MAIN STAGE, with *Sponsored by Drake's Carpets of Bristol* in smaller lettering underneath. Beyond it, the cricket ground was dark, the stages and various tents closed up for the night.

Beyond the cricket ground, the road arced slightly to the left, and farther up on the right Lucy finally spotted what she was after. A fish n' chips sign creaked in a light breeze, and from the lights inside, she could tell the shop was still open.

She was about halfway there when she heard a soft voice from over a hedgerow on the left-hand side.

Lucy slowed, sure she recognised it as the voice of Mark Bale. She crept closer to the hedge, feeling like an idiot for eavesdropping, but at the same time unable to curb her curiosity.

'...and the boys are fine, although I wish Trev would set his sights a little higher. I'm still looking into properties in London since sales have picked up there, so he might be interested in management if we could get a store going. The Bristol store is well on the way to open in the spring. It's all well and good, but it means I'll have to take on more staff to cope with the demand. Really, I never thought it would get this big. I only wish you were here to see what we've made. You'd have been so proud....'

With a lurch in her gut, Lucy realised what she was hearing. She walked a little farther on and saw an open gate leading into a small graveyard. A torch identified Mark Bale as he sat by a grave near to the hedgerow Lucy had stood behind. She wanted to listen longer, but her morals wouldn't let her, so she hurried across the street so that Mark wouldn't see her and then continued to the chip shop.

When she came out a few minutes later and crossed the street to the graveyard, the gate was closed and Mark was gone. Far up ahead, she just caught a glimpse of him walking briskly up the street.

As soon as he was out of sight, Lucy slipped through the gate and pulled out her smartphone. Using the torch function, she quickly identified the grave next to which Mark had been crouched.

Mary Susan Bale
March 1ˢᵗ 1976 to December 20ᵗʰ 2005
Loving wife and mother
Taken from us too soon
Forever in our thoughts

A tear dribbled down Lucy's cheek. Fourteen years ago, Mark's wife and Dan and Tarquin's mother had died just before Christmas.

And here Lucy was eating fish n' chips on her own on a dark street while her parents were eating together somewhere nearby.

'What's wrong with me?' she muttered, putting her torch away and standing up.

She no longer had an appetite, so she headed back to the holiday park and put her fish n' chips in a plastic bag to save for tomorrow. No doubt one of her parents would want them in the morning if they were having another Christmas party together. She sat down on a sofa in the living room area and did an internet search.

It wasn't hard to find news reports relating to Mary Bale's death. According to one local newspaper, she had died in a car accident on the Camelford to Bodmin road, her car struck by a lorry that was reportedly driving too wide around a blind bend. Mercifully she had died instantly.

Lucy sat numbly on the sofa for a long time. She fiddled with her phone for a while, wanting first to call her parents, then to call Melanie for some advice, and finally deciding against all of it. She switched on the TV but she looked through it, taking nothing in. An hour after a documentary began, she could barely remember what it was about.

It was nearly midnight when she heard her parents' voices from outside. The most surprising thing was that there were other voices with them, but just when Lucy was thinking Alan and Valerie had brought a party back with them, they wished goodnight to two people Lucy overheard were called Jen and Mick, who soon after went into an adjacent tent.

The zip whizzed, and Valerie appeared, clearly worse for wear, a piece of tinsel tied around her neck and a plastic reindeer pocking out of her jacket pocket. Alan had a string of silver bells tied to one foot, and as he turned to take off his shoes, Lucy saw a piece of paper still taped to his back. On it was scrawled "Mike from *Monsters Inc*."

'Oh, there you are, dear,' Valerie said, noticing Lucy standing by the kitchen counter, watching them. 'Are you going to scold us for being back so late? Honestly, I'd do it over again to hear your dad slaughter that song from *Lion King* at karaoke just one more time.'

'Says the woman who cheats at Twister,' Alan said, slumping down onto a sofa. 'I had that left-foot-green until you poked your finger in my ribs.'

'You were nowhere near,' Valerie said, slumping down beside him. Then, looking up at Lucy, she said, 'So how was your night, dear?'

Lucy smiled. 'Enlightening,' she said. Then, feeling a sudden rush of happiness, she slumped down on the sofa, squeezing between them.

'I'm sorry,' she said. 'I just want you to know that I'm so glad I came. And … that I love you both so much.'

17

PREPARATIONS

'Reheated chips all right for breakfast?' Lucy called into the curtained area that was her parents' bedroom. The only response was a change in the timbre of Alan's snoring. 'I'll take that as a "yes" then.'

She made them both a cup of coffee and left the bag of chips next to the microwave, with a cheeky post-it note beside the start button with "press me" written on it. Then, leaving them to sleep, she headed up to the village with a newfound sense of enthusiasm.

It was not yet nine o'clock so most of the shops were still closed, but at the cricket ground she found Ellie, clipboard in hand, directing a large lorry as it awkwardly reversed in through the car park gates.

'Good morning!' Ellie greeted her. 'How are your parents bearing up this morning? I imagine your dad's a bit hoarse. Tell him I want a free carpet or I'll upload the video of him slaughtering *Living on a Prayer* to the internet.'

Lucy smiled. 'Will do. They were still, um, relaxing when I came out.'

'That's great. They don't have to worry about anything until it all kicks off. At the moment we're mostly just waiting for things to arrive.'

'What's in the lorry?'

Ellie winked. 'A big surprise. Very big. It'll blow everyone away. Well, unless it blows away. We've been pretty lucky with the weather, haven't we?'

Lucy nodded. 'Well, I suppose so. You could almost play cricket out here today. A shame it's not going to snow, but then I wouldn't expect it on the Cornish coast.' She shrugged. 'I've heard all it does is rain.'

'Have you seen the forecast? Snow is due on Christmas Eve. Ah, here we are.' She pointed at a van just pulling in behind the still-reversing lorry. 'That's what this lot is for. Come on, help me unload.'

Lucy followed Ellie over to the van as the lorry finally came to a stop. The driver climbed out and led both women around to the back.

'Snow shovels,' the driver said with a grin, pulling open the back doors to reveal stacks of bright red plastic shovels tied together in groups of ten. 'Not sure what you're going to use them for if doesn't snow.'

'It'll snow,' Ellie said. 'Trust me. I have a sixth sense for such things.'

'Well, I'll take your word for it,' the driver said.

Lucy helped them unload the shovels, carrying

them around to a storage shed next to the cricket pavilion.

'If that snow came early, it would be ideal,' Ellie said. 'We really need it in place for the snowman competition.'

'A snowman competition?'

'Can't be Christmas without one.' Ellie gave a sudden sigh. 'A shame I won't be here to see it.'

'No?'

'I have to go back up to Scotland on Christmas Eve morning. My youngest son is getting married on Christmas Day.'

'Oh, congratulations!'

Ellie smiled. 'It's about time. A shame I haven't married off my older son yet, but it'll happen eventually. He's too nice not to find someone.' She gave Lucy a gentle nudge in the ribs with her elbow. 'If you fancy coming up with me, I'm sure he'd be glad to meet you….'

Lucy couldn't help but neigh a sudden gasping laugh. She looked at Ellie and frowned. 'Oh, I doubt that.'

Ellie frowned and patted her on the arm. 'You know, that really is a fearsome laugh, but you're overreacting a little.'

'I'm really not. My dad said it could sink ships, and it has actually crashed a car. It's also caused at least three relationships to end, and labeled me with endless nicknames through school.'

'I can imagine. You know what, though? You should just let it out. Every time you laugh, you try to shun it, cut it off. Just let it go. If you do, I bet you'll find it's not nearly as bad as you think.'

'I'll take your word for it.'

'You know, you remind me a lot of my son's fiancée. Poor girl had a terrible time of it before they met, idiot ex-boyfriend and all that. She didn't have much confidence either. Do you know what people like—men and women, of any age, even if they don't know it—more than anything else in a possible partner?'

'I'm sure you're going to tell me….'

'Of course I am. Confidence. That and positivity. None of us are perfect, are we?'

An image of Elizabeth Trevellian flashed up in Lucy's mind. The girl could certainly do with being a bit nicer, even if she had the looks part totally nailed down.

'I suppose not.'

Ellie nudged Lucy again. 'Well, I suppose men are a bit fallible to the old damsel-in-distress routine. My poor lad had no chance once he laid eyes on Maggie, bless her heart. He was head over heels before he even knew it.'

'Sounds like love at first sight.'

Ellie shrugged. 'More or less. Christmas has a way of bringing these emotions out a little too. You never know, you might find someone yourself if we get a decent blanket of snow.'

Lucy gave an indignant frown. 'I'm not looking.'

'Are you sure about that?'

'Absolutely.'

Ellie offered a sly grin. 'Well, you just carry on not looking. But to be on the safe side, I'd stay away from the fudge shop.'

Lucy felt her cheeks plume with heat. 'What's that supposed to mean?'

'Nothing at all.' Ellie winked again then patted Lucy on the arm. 'I have to get back to sorting out this rabble, but any time you want a chat … come and find me.'

As Ellie marched off, waving her clipboard and shouting at the lorry driver who had climbed out of his cab and was sipping from a flask as steam rose around his face, Lucy headed back to the high street. *Stay away from the fudge shop.* It felt like a challenge. Dan was the local dentist; he probably wouldn't be there anyway. And part of her wanted to speak to Mark, if only to let him know she had overheard him talking by his wife's grave and to offer her condolences.

Back along the high street, right up to the turning down to Tintagel Castle, a flurry of industry had begun. Half an hour earlier the street had been silent besides a couple of dog-walkers. Now it was a swarm of activity. Three lorries had pulled up, and a man in a construction worker's hat was delivering a speech to a group of shop workers. Mark was standing near the front, his arms folded, but as Lucy approached, the speaking man clapped his hands together and everyone began to disperse.

Lucy found herself standing outside the fudge shop as Mark returned, absently picking off a piece of lint from a brown apron with the BALE'S FUDGE AND CONFECTIONERY logo printed on it.

'Oh, all right, Frances? How are you today?'

Lucy blushed again. 'Please call me Lucy. Only my dad calls me Frances.'

'Haha, sure, as you like. I heard from Tarquin that your mum and dad had a good night down The Lighthouse.'

Lucy grinned. 'It looked like it. They were snoring away when I came out. What's going on here?'

'Part of the transformation. From the twenty-third through to New Year, Tintagel's high street will be transformed into an international Christmas market.'

Lucy felt a little tingle of excitement. 'Seriously?'

'Every business is involved. Over the last six months we've all been in contact with European versions of our own shops and making arrangements for them to come over. We have confectionery from France, trinkets from Spain, even art from Italy up at the gallery there. I'm sticking to fudge, of course. I'm partnered with a German fudge maker called Klaus Berenstein, who's bringing ingredients from the Black Forest and Rhine Valley to give my fudge a little international kick.'

Lucy shook her head. 'No way my dad's going to survive this without a heart attack,' she said.

'A good job Ellie's here. She's an expert at maintaining a balance, apparently. Cliff walks, Christmas-themed line-dancing, even snow-aerobics. They're all on the schedule. I don't know how they do it. All I'm planning to do is cook and sell a ton of fudge.'

'Is it hard?' Lucy asked. 'You know, I have no idea how to cook fudge.'

'Easy when you have the gear,' Mark said. 'Listen, my stall's not scheduled for setting up until after lunch, so this morning is all about cooking as much of the stuff as I can in preparation. Why don't you come in and help me? I'll show you how it's done.'

Lucy hesitated only a moment. What was it Ellie had said about confidence and positivity? Learning something new … that was being positive, wasn't it?

'Sure, why not?' she said.

Mark smiled. 'Great.' He patted her on the shoulder. 'Dan's just getting the sugar from out the back.'

18

FUDGE MAKING

It was too late to back out having already agreed. Lucy hoped her cheeks weren't red enough to cause anyone temporary blindness as Mark led her into the shop, calling out as he did so.

'Dan, we have a guest! Can you grab another apron?'

Inside, the shop was petite, with only room for a dozen or so people standing shoulder to shoulder to browse the various shelves loaded with an assortment of fudge-based confectionery and other local products, from packets of biscuits and shortcake to racks of postcards and pamphlet-sized local history books. The main counter had a glass front to allow customers to view the mountains of homemade fudge inside, everything from plain vanilla to colourful fruit, nut, or candy-infused flavours. Behind the counter, the shop was much warmer from heat coming out of the attached kitchen, a relief to Lucy because she had already begun to sweat at the thought of encountering Dan. As Mark led her through a hanging curtain into a clinically clean kitchen area filled with huge stainless steel cooking pots and wide work surfaces, Dan came through a door that led into a storeroom piled high with bags of ingredients.

'Well, hello again,' Dan said.

Lucy tried to summon a simmering anger that might suppress the obvious attraction she felt, but Dan had such an easy smile to go with his natural good looks that she found herself just gazing at him as he held out an apron. He wore one of his own over a t-shirt tight enough to display far more muscle than any dentist Lucy had ever been misfortunate enough to visit. His hair, short but appearing wind-ruffled, had blond highlights and his eyes were as brown as the fudge. He smiled, revealing the kind of teeth only a dentist should have.

'You really should put this on. The sugar gets pretty hot and it can burn little holes in your clothes. I've ruined a ton of decent t-shirts.'

'Couldn't you patch them?' Lucy said in a strained high-pitched voice, immediately realising what a stupid thing it was to say and then coughing out a couple of choked laughs as though to cover it.

Dan winced. 'Um, I suppose I could, but I just donate them to Tarquin. He's into quilting. He specialises in using old surf gear.'

Lucy stared. 'Quilting? Isn't that what

grandmothers do?' She barked another whooping cough laugh then slapped her hand over her mouth as sweat began to roll like breakers off the Atlantic coast. She quite literally wanted to be anywhere else in the world right now, but as Mark came behind her, she found herself trapped between them.

'His grandmother taught him,' Mark said. 'Last year he won a regional prize for one with a design which represented the effects of pollution on local beaches. He sells them for five grand apiece. Sometimes I think I'm in the wrong business.'

Despite her surprise at Tarquin's unlikely hobby, Lucy was sweating so bad she wanted to curl up and die. She just gave a frantic nod, wondering how she could escape without losing her mind.

Dan was clearly amused at her obvious discomfort. 'Is this your first time to make fudge?' he asked.

'Yes,' Lucy croaked, deciding it was perhaps best not to add any more detail for fear of further embarrassing herself.

''There's really nothing to it,' Mark said. 'It's eighty percent sugar. We only use Cornish sugar, of course. No imported rubbish.'

Lucy frowned. 'Cornish sugar?' Certain Mark was having a joke with her, she slapped a hand over her mouth to stop herself laughing, even though it was more out of nervousness than anything else. She didn't think she'd ever felt less like laughing in her entire life, but her body was betraying her at the exact wrong time. 'Where?' Croak. 'How?' Wheeze. 'Cornish *sugar?*'

'Eden Project,' Dan said. 'They have these huge bio-domes, and they grow all sorts of tropical stuff. How long are you around? If you like, I could take you down there after Christmas. It's an interesting place.'

Lucy was certain she was dehydrating as the sweat came faster than ever, soaking her collar. Had Dan just suggested doing something together? Like a date?

'I'm sure my parents would love to see it,' she muttered, as Mark, frowning, peered at a thermostat control on the wall.

'Well, I suppose we could take them too,' Dan said, sounding a little disappointed as Lucy glanced behind her, wondering if the huge cauldrons were big enough to curl up in. There were perhaps worse ways to escape the suffocating awkwardness of this situation than being cooked into a rather poor-tasting fudge. She gritted her teeth, determined that not another single word would come from her mouth unless it had her brain's all-clear first.

'Okay, kids, let's get this batch underway,' Mark said, grinning at Dan before turning to Lucy and offering her a wink.

As Mark and Dan shuffled into production readiness, Lucy felt a sharp sense of relief that she could settle back into being an observer. Hopefully, if they got fully engrossed, she could quietly slip back and away out of the shop, then find a hole somewhere to hide in until Christmas was over—

'Lucy, grab the other side of this, please.'

Dan was looking at her with one eyebrow raised, waiting for her to follow his instructions. He was leaning down, with one hand on a corner of the huge sack of sugar at his feet.

'Excuse me...?'

'You take the other side. We'll dump it in together.'

'That doesn't sound very scientific.'

Dan laughed. 'Leave all the complicated stuff to Dad. We're just his worker bees.'

'Sugar in first,' Mark said, lining up a pot big enough to hold a couple of decent-sized turkeys. He nodded as Dan and Lucy poured the sugar inside. 'Perfect,' he said. 'I'll start this warming while you show Lucy what we need next.'

Dan led Lucy out into the storeroom and over to a towering, double-doored industrial-sized fridge. Lucy was glad for the cool air as he pulled the doors open and handed her a heavy plastic carton.

'Clotted cream,' he said. 'And I'll bring the butter.'

'How much is in this?'

'Three kilograms.' Dan grinned. 'Wholesale size. So, is your name really Frances Drake?'

Lucy, who had been slowly cooling off after her litany of faux pas, felt a renewed hot flush. She wished she were closer to the fridge, but Dan had got in the way of the flow of cool air.

'Well, kind of,' she said, feeling a certain comfort

109

in the familiarity of her upbringing and its curses. 'It's Frances Lucinda Scullion-Drake.'

'Brutal.' Dan smiled. 'But I like it. It's interesting. I'm Daniel Bale. I sound like a make of tractor.'

'No, you don't. It's … smooth. Easy to say.' The words felt stupid, but Lucy had reached the infinity point for her embarrassment and there was nowhere else to go.

'But it's got no spark to it, not like yours.'

'You actually like my name? You know what they called me in school?'

'I'm not sure I dare guess.'

'In primary I was Onion Duck. One of the kids in my class had a dad who was a chef and he mistook Scullion for scallion. Of course, it stuck. They always do, don't they?'

'It's school,' Dan said. 'What about secondary?'

Vaguely aware that Dan seemed genuinely interested and that the confessional nature of her words was taking away some of her awkwardness, Lucy said, 'Onion Duck was a bit clunky for the morons in my secondary, so people started calling me Goosey Lucy. Apparently I looked and sounded like one. Even though I preferred Lucy to Frances, which all the teachers called me, from about the third year I started going as Frankie. I never liked it though. Since school I've always gone as Lucy. My dad still calls me Frances, but my mum will call me whatever I tell her to call me. She's like that. She's a researcher in a science lab, and is a bit like a computer program. You can program her to behave in a certain way, and she'll do whatever is most efficient. I like Lucy, so she calls me Lucy.'

Dan smiled. Lucy felt a sudden returning hot flush as she realised she had laid her soul bare in front of someone she had barely met, but Dan didn't seem to mind. He actually seemed interested. 'My dad always calls me Dan,' he said. 'From as young as I can remember. My mum, though, she used to call me Daniel,' Dan said. 'Before—'

'This fudge won't cook itself,' Mark called through the storeroom door. 'I'm happy for your little mother's meeting, but can you hurry up back there?'

Dan laughed. Lucy started laughing too before she could think to catch herself. She cut it off with a sharp gasp that came out like a burp, then slapped her hand over her mouth, nearly dropping the cream as she caught the container in the crutch of one elbow.

'Don't mess with the fudge,' Dan whispered, leaning close. 'Dad is pretty particular about the way it gets made. And by the way, don't have so much of a complex about your laugh. You've just got to make sure there's enough background noise to drown it out.'

She had been warming to his character and was sure he didn't mean it the way it came out, but even so, the words cut deep to Lucy's bones. She turned away from him and staggered back through the doorway with her load of cream, trying to concentrate on something else.

Mark was standing by the cauldron, a cricket bat in hand. For a moment Lucy thought she'd made a terrible error of judgement and had found herself in the middle of a horror movie, before noticing the melted sugar dripping off the bat's lower edge.

'Quick, dump it in,' Mark said, nodding at the massive pan.

Lucy pulled the lid off the clotted cream and held it up while Dan scooped the gloopy substance into the pan. He then unwrapped the butter and dropped it in.

'Stir it,' Mark said to Lucy, holding out the cricket bat. 'Don't stop, and make sure not to forget the edges and the bottom. We have to keep it consistent.'

'Is this really a cricket bat?' Lucy said, dipping it into the cauldron and pulling it through the glutinous mixture.

'It is indeed,' Mark said. 'Obviously it's a bit thinner because I had to strip off all the linseed-infused covering, but it makes a great wooden spoon. And while I can't prove it, I think the willow adds a certain something to the flavour.'

'Cornish willow,' Dan added. 'Came from a tree on the Camel Estuary. Dad likes to keep everything local.'

Mark held up a plastic beaker and shook it before tossing its contents into the pan. 'Even the salt comes from a farm in the Isles of Scilly. When the sign says it's Cornish-made, I like to mean it.'

Lucy, pushing and drawing on the mixture, was starting to tire. Dan reached for the bat and she gratefully handed it over.

'It's exhausting,' she said.

Mark smiled. 'How do you think the lad here got

his arms? I had him help me right through school, stirring these vats of an evening. Kept away the bullies and drew the ladies, didn't it, Dan?'

Dan shrugged. 'I suppose.'

Lucy, struggling with her feelings, was unable to avoid considering Dan's brief smile as smug. Her feelings were like a see-saw, bouncing up and down. At one moment Dan was a handsome, dedicated son, at the next he was insulting and full of himself. Even so, she couldn't help notice the power he had as he pushed the cricket bat through the mix.

Mark dipped a handheld sugar thermometer into the mix and held it up. 'One hundred and eight Celsius,' he said. 'We need just a little more. 'One-one-six is the sweet spot. A little less if you want it more granular, a little more for creamier. Here in Cornwall we're all at a pretty standard one-one-six. Gives the region's fudge a similarity in its taste. Similarity means familiarity. We want people who want Cornish fudge to come to Cornwall, not head down to their local Tescos and buy some rubbish made in a factory in Sussex.'

'Time for the ingredients, Dad?' Dan asked. 'What's this one going to be?'

'Walnut,' Mark said, holding up a bag. With a grin, he added, 'From a tree down in St. Ives.' Turning to Lucy he added, 'With hard ingredients like these, we add them near the end and just stir them in. With something we want to mix in, such as chocolate, we'd add it a bit earlier on so that it can properly infuse. To get that lovely marbling effect, we might pour the basic mixture first and then the mix over the top, but it all depends what we're adding. I have about ten basic flavours that are popular, but the rest I'll make depending on what ingredients I can get my hands on.'

'It's almost scientific,' Lucy said.

'Ah, it's easy really,' Mark said. 'My grandfather originally started this shop. He passed it to my father, who left it to me. Three generations, and I hope one of the boys will make it a fourth. My father was a very local man, though. Wasn't interested in expanding the business. I've been looking at opening stores in both London and Bristol.'

'I remember you saying.'

The words were out before Lucy could stop herself. She clapped a hand over her mouth, wondering if there was still time to jump into the vat and be melted down into fudge.

'Did I tell you about it in the van on the way down? I don't remember—'

Lucy decided to come clean. 'I ... I ... overheard you. Um, yesterday. By your ... your wife's grave. I'm sorry, I was walking to the chip shop, and I heard a voice....'

Lucy was glad the fudge wasn't going to be tomato flavour, otherwise Mark might have thrown her cheeks in. She stood between them, feeling like a Peeping Tom caught red-handed.

'Well, yes, I go over there every anniversary,' Mark said, looking down, clearly upset. 'Dan, lad, would you mind finishing this off for me?'

'Sure, Dad.'

Without looking back up, Mark pulled off his gloves and apron and went out into the shop. Even though Dan gave her a pat on the shoulder, as though to reassure her that she hadn't just committed some great social atrocity, Lucy wished the ground would swallow her up.

19

VISITOR

'So, you're a spy as well as a historical navy commander,' Dan said, giving the mixture one more stir before checking the thermometer again. 'You have quite the C.V.'

'I didn't mean to spy on him. I thought he was talking to someone. I only stopped for a minute. Once I realised he was in the graveyard, I went on my way.'

'He's never got over her death,' Dan said. 'We almost lost the shop because Dad could barely work for six months after it happened. Trev and me did all the prep at night and we had a local lady come in to work the till during the day. Dad was either in the pub or wandering the cliffs. There were days when I didn't think he'd make it through.'

'But he did?'

'Eventually, he did. He pulled himself together and carried on for our sakes. He feels almost as bad for letting us down as he did for what happened to

Mum. You see, he blames himself. It was a Sunday. He always went to the wholesaler outside Bodmin on a Sunday, but that weekend the weather was fine and Mum told him to go off fishing, take a break. She offered to do the supply run and a lorry hit her on the way back.'

'That's awful.'

'It wasn't Dad's fault, of course. The driver had been drinking, and took the curve so wide he was practically in the other lane. The Camelford to Bodmin road is a shocker, though, full of blind corners and hidden dips. There have been loads of accidents there but we're still waiting for it to be straightened. You can go via Kennard's House and take the A30, of course, but that adds half an hour to the journey, and on a weekend the traffic can be terrible.'

'The circumstances, though ... I can see why it hurt him so much.'

'They were so happy, my parents. By then Trev had come out, and Dad knew I wanted to go into dentistry and therefore not take over the business, but they were totally fine about everything. Dad wanted to use Trev on his marketing campaigns, and he said he'd wait until I had kids and then pass the shop on to them. My parents were so close, and they were always so positive about everything. Then my mum died, and for the next year everything went dark. We almost lost the business, but even worse was that we almost lost Dad.'

'But you came through it?'

'That closeness between us all … it was damaged, but it came through in the end. We survived. It's an unhappy memory, but we're through it.'

'I'm sorry I brought it up.'

'The anniversary of Mum's death was yesterday. Dad's always a bit morose at this time of the year, but he'll be fine.'

Almost on cue, Mark appeared in the doorway. He had his apron and his gloves back on, and his cheeks were flushed as though he'd just had a quick glass of pick-me-up.

'Haven't you got it out and in the trays yet?' he said with a grin. 'Come on, Dan, hurry up or it'll taste like it was made in Devon.' Turning to Lucy, he said, 'I'm sorry about that. You caught me unawares.'

'I'm sorry if you thought I was eavesdropping,' Lucy said. 'I didn't mean to.'

'It's quite all right. I imagine Dan has explained. This time of year is always a little tough, but it's Christmas. My wife would never have wanted us moping around. She was always the first to get the god-awful jumpers on and start singing the Crimbo songs.'

'She certainly was,' Dan said. 'She would have loved what's happening here this year.'

'And we'll make it the best Christmas we can, in her memory,' Mark said. 'Come on, let's get this poured.'

Lucy stepped back while Mark and Dan lifted the cauldron off the heat and poured the fudge into three wide trays. As they finished the third, Mark turned to Lucy.

'Grab one of those plastic spatulas and spread it out,' he said. 'Make sure it's even, right to the corners.'

Lucy did as she was told. When the melted fudge was ready, Dan pulled on a pair of the oven gloves and carried the fudge out to the storeroom. Lucy thought he was going to the fridge, but instead he opened a back door and stepped out into a small conservatory.

'Local refrigeration unit,' Mark told Lucy. 'Coastal winds. Don't tell health and safety but I've been doing it this way for years. Takes about two hours to get it perfect. You don't want it freezing cold, but if it's too warm it'll be difficult to cut.'

'How long will it last?'

Mark shrugged. 'You can put it in sealed confectionery bags and it'll last for months, but I want it tasting fresh. Anything over four days gets bagged up and donated to a local children's charity.' He grinned. 'Orphans from North Cornwall have the worst teeth in the country.'

'But the biggest smiles,' Dan added as he came back inside. 'Right, we're done.'

'I put the kettle on just before,' Mark said. 'Let's go get a brew and have something to eat. Sure I can pull something from the rack to make room for what we've just made.'

They headed back into the shop. Mark had

turned the sign around to OPEN, but there were no customers yet.

'In the summer we have a couple of tables outside,' Mark said. 'And we get the coffee machine going. We could expand into a café, but that would take business away from the other cafés along the high street. As it is, I supply three of them with fudge. Round here, hard competition doesn't help anyone. We're all friends, and we help each other out.'

'I wish it was like that in Bristol,' Lucy said, as Mark handed her a plate. 'I work in a travel agency. There's another one three doors down which is constantly trying to undercut us. It gets tiring.'

'That doesn't surprise me,' Mark said, instructing Dan to pour coffees from a filter jug. 'You like it black or white? Sugar? Come on, take your pick of the fudge in the rack. Anything you'd like.'

Lucy caught Dan's eye as he poured coffee into a mug with the shop's logo on it. He gave her a smile. The anger she had felt for him melted away and she realised how nice it would be to wake up to see that smile first thing in the morning.

'Come on, girl, fill your boots.'

Dan smiled again as Lucy turned to the fudge rack behind the shop's counter. It was loaded high with the most wonderful, pungent fudge, in more flavours than she had realised were possible. She didn't want Dan to think she was a pig, though. With a shy smile, she picked up one small piece of vanilla and another small piece of toffee-chocolate. As she retreated to the table where Dan had set their coffees down, Mark shook his head.

'Either you're being polite or you're being disrespectful to my fudge,' he said. 'Come on, girl, you're skin over bones. Need to get some meat on that figure.' As Dan laughed, Mark took the plate from Lucy and loaded it with a couple of handfuls of fudge. Lucy stared in dismay at the mound of nearly pure sugar, even though it looked and smelled delicious.

'Merry Christmas,' Mark said, taking a small plateful of his own and setting it down. At Lucy's shocked look, he added, 'I have an excuse. I'm old. You don't.'

'I'll keep Lucy company,' Dan said, sitting down beside her and putting a plate as equally loaded as her own down in front of him.

'Thanks,' she whispered.

'Tuck in,' Mark said, lifting his coffee mug. 'Merry Christmas, everyone. And Lucy, thanks for helping us out. You have a knack for it.'

'Ah, it was easy,' Lucy said, smiling.

'If you're tired of the travel industry, I could probably do with a decent manager for the store I'm planning to open in Bristol,' Mark said. 'You know, Dan would be nearby if you needed help. His dental practice is up in Bristol, did he tell you that?'

'Um, no—'

'It's on Queens Road, just past the Clifton Triangle,' he said. 'I gave up trying to fix all the teeth

Dad was ruining in Cornwall. Far too much like hard work.'

Lucy stared. It was barely a stones' throw from her travel agent. He had probably only missed out on an invite to Melanie's Christmas mash-up by fifty metres.

'I didn't know that,' Lucy said. 'Um, I'll certainly give it some thought.' Even as she said it, the idea of managing a pretty little fudge store seemed more appealing than she might have expected. And if Dan was nearby … the possibilities didn't bear considering.

'It's harder work than it looks,' Mark said. Then, grinning as he picked up a piece of fudge, he added, 'But it certainly has its perks. Go on, eat up.'

Shyly, Lucy picked up a piece of fudge and put it into her mouth. It was thick and creamy, so sweet she felt lightheaded. She had just begun to chew it when the shop door swung open, and with a dramatic flourish, Elizabeth Trevellian strode inside.

Balanced on Elizabeth's head was a wide-brimmed hat which would have looked more appropriate at Ascot Races. Below it, a designer jacket that had probably cost more than Lucy's father's car.

'Oh, Daniel, there you are. You know, for someone so striking you are rather elusive. We'll have lunch today, won't we? Just to talk. I'm only interested in clearing the air, and, well, clearing the path for future opportunities.'

Behind her, the two photographers were standing in the doorway, one on his knees with a camera, the other holding up the reflective sheet. As a sudden gust of wind caught the sheet, causing both men to scramble to catch it before the wind took it away down the high street, Elizabeth seemed to notice Lucy for the first time.

'Oh! It's you. The barking girl. I hope you don't bite like you bark, or we'll all be in trouble.' As Lucy tried to chew around the thick lump of fudge, Elizabeth started to laugh. Her assistant's camera turned in Lucy's direction just as Elizabeth said, 'Well, Daniel, I see you've found a way to shut her up.'

20

VOCAL TRAINING

WITH HER BAG OF FUDGE SWINGING AT HER SIDE, Lucy headed back to the holiday park, wondering if her star was in the ascent or firmly back into a nosedive. Elizabeth Trevellian had flourished and twisted and flown back out of the door with a promise to track Dan down later before anyone had got off a single word in reply. Lucy, feeling the mood had been broken as both Dan and Mark looked uncomfortable after the woman's sudden appearance, made an excuse about checking on her parents and then got out of there as fast as she could.

Not before Mark had bagged up her leftover fudge as a present for her parents, though. Lucy, wanting to clear both Dan and Elizabeth out of her mind, was already wondering how she would sneak the confectionery past her mother.

When she arrived, her parents were sitting around a picnic table on the wooden terrace outside their tent, mugs of coffee in hand and the remains of Lucy's fish n' chips on a plate in front of them. Down in the valley, the holiday park was free from the wind which hassled the clifftop, and even though it was cold enough that her parents were wearing jackets as well as the now-required Christmas hats, it wasn't unpleasant.

Lucy took a seat beside them and dropped the packet of fudge down on the table. 'How are you both feeling? Mum, I got you a present.'

Valerie stared at the bag of fudge. 'Oh, dear, I couldn't possibly eat all that—'

'Dad can help you then.'

'Sure,' Alan said, scooping up the bag with a wide grin. Glancing at Valerie, he said, 'Love, what a wonderful daughter we have.'

'Just don't eat it all at once,' Valerie said, throwing Lucy a frustrated look. Then, just as she looked about to say something else, the door to the tent beside theirs opened and two middle-aged people emerged.

'Oh, there's Jen and Mick,' Alan said. 'Guys, come and have a piece of fudge. This here's my daughter, Frances. Love, put the kettle on for Jen and Mick, won't you?'

As Lucy dutifully headed for the tent, her parents began a series of backslaps and high-fives with their apparent new best friends.

'I've never seen *The Final Countdown* done with air-guitar like that,' Mick said, slapping Alan on the back. 'Legendary.'

'Ah, you made a fine organ player. Pub again tonight?'

'Wouldn't miss it. Merry Christmas, compadres.'

A couple of minutes later, when Lucy returned with a freshly brewed pot of coffee and a couple more mugs, Mick was arguing with Alan about the rules of Twister while Jen was trying to interest Valerie in peer-reviewing a scientific article on freshwater algae. Lucy gave them a wave, then announced she was heading up to the cricket ground.

At least they were enjoying themselves, she thought, as she walked up the steep farm lane to the high street. And part of her was enjoying herself too, even if her emotions were still clouding her judgment. Did she like Dan or not? Had there been anything in their exchange this morning to suggest he liked her too, or was it an idea she should just give up on? Drink as much hot chocolate, eat as much fudge as she could, and laugh as loud as possible until everyone around her was scared away.

Sounded like a plan.

At the cricket ground the stage set-up was finished, and beneath an awning a group of technicians were setting up sound and light equipment. Ellie was standing outside the pavilion, clipboard in hand, giving out instructions to workmen as they came and went.

'Good morning,' Ellie called cheerfully, waving her clipboard at Lucy as she approached. 'How are your parents again this morning? Great night in the pub last night. Warn them not to peak too early. We

126

have an internationally renowned Christmas pudding chef arriving this afternoon.'

'I'll do my best. I'm afraid I left them with a bag full of fudge.'

Ellie shrugged. 'Worse ways to spend a morning,' she said. 'Did you go to Bale's? Best fudge I've ever tasted. Mark Bale's a magician.' Then, with a wink, she added, 'Plus, his older son's a dish.'

Lucy hoped she wasn't blushing as she said, 'I hadn't noticed.'

'Sure you hadn't. I'm guessing there's no special person up in Bristol, otherwise he'd be here with you.'

Lucy shook her head. 'I'm as single as the day I was born.'

'And what better time to be single than on Christmas, at the biggest party in the south of England. It's almost perfect.' Like a rain god, Ellie suddenly spread her hands and peered upward. 'Come on, just a flake. Let me know you're ready.'

Lucy almost laughed but caught herself just in time. 'I really can't see it snowing,' she said. 'And anyway, if it did, there'd be chaos.'

Ellie turned and waved a hand. 'Da-da!'

In a line by the edge of the cricket ground were five mini-buses. 'What are they?' Lucy asked.

'Four-wheel-drive, snow tires with chains in the back if necessary, and they even come with drivers trained in snow conditions.' She grinned. 'They're Swiss. Imported. They promised to wear full traditional dress too.'

'What are they for?'

'That's our taxi service to and from Tintagel over Christmas. Each bus will operate in a loop around all the designated camp grounds and parking areas for non-residents. Trust me, when that snow comes, we'll be ready.'

'And if it doesn't?'

'Win-win. The drivers also happen to be a trained theatrical group. They're going to do a musical version of *Heidi* on Christmas Eve.'

'And who's going to play Heidi?'

Ellie rolled her eyes. 'Oh, Lucy, my dear, so presumptive. Do all taxi drivers have to be men?'

As if on cue, the pavilion door opened and a woman Lucy could only describe as a walking stereotype appeared, stooping low to avoid hitting her head. At least six feet six inches tall, she had thick blonde hair to her waist that was twisted into plaits as thick as rope. A red skirt top hung over white leggings. She even appeared to be wearing clogs.

'Ah, Frederika,' Ellie said, waving the towering behemoth of a woman over. 'This is my friend Lucy.'

'Charmed,' Frederika said in a thick Swiss-German accent. 'It is my pleasure to make your acquaintance.'

As a hand the size of a bear's paw enveloped her own, Lucy couldn't stop herself from laughing. As she clapped a hand over her mouth to cut it off, Frederika frowned at Ellie.

'What is dis sound? You have the lungs problem?'

Lucy shook her head. 'No....'

'Then you have de gift.'

'What gift?'

Frederika leaned back her head and spread her arms. Lucy stared as an incredible roar came from the woman's lungs. It began as a single note, then rose up and down, turning into a yodel. Halfway across the cricket ground, the engine of a tractor cut out, and a group of workmen brought into a hearty round of applause.

The sound came to a gentle halt. Frederika turned to Lucy. 'Now, it is your turn.'

Lucy shook her head. 'I can't do that—'

Frederika's bear paw struck her on the back, making her cough. 'Sing, woman, sing! Let out the sound given to you at birth! Make it glorious!'

Surely this was some sort of joke. Lucy stared at her, feeling a tickle of sweat on her brow. Then Frederika slapped her on the back again. Closing her eyes, she tried to make some kind of sound come out, but all that emerged was a whiny sound like a vibrating water pipe.

Ellie had added a grimace to her frown. She gave Lucy a well-wishing pat on the back again, then shrugged.

'She is untrained,' Frederika said. 'I will make it my responsibility. We have a space in de musical that needs to be filled. You are the one.'

'I can't sing,' Lucy said.

'It is more than just singing. It is expression. It is baring your soul to the world. You, my dear, have a fractured soul, and this is the best of all. You will astound the world on Christmas night!'

Like Romeo calling to Juliet, or perhaps threatening to pull the entire balcony down, Frederika lifted one arm dramatically into the air. She stared at the sky while Lucy and Ellie waited for her to speak again. Then, with a slow nod, she said, as though to someone neither of them could see, 'Yes. I will train her.'

'I should perhaps be getting back,' Lucy said, but Frederika appeared not to hear her, and turned, taking Lucy's arm and guiding her back toward the cricket pavilion while a bemused Ellie just shrugged. 'I will show you ze techniques,' she said. 'I will show you how you can free the magic you keep locked inside you. Are you ready to astound ze world?'

Lucy just shrugged. She wanted to run and hide, but something about this larger-than-life woman was addictive.

'I'll give it a go,' she said.

21

TEST FLIGHT

AN HOUR LATER, HER THROAT SO SORE SHE WAS barely able to croak, Lucy emerged from the changing room where Frederika had attempted to teach her to yodel and went through into the pavilion bar, where Ellie was stirring a vat of hot chocolate for workmen lining up to drink. A few of them gave her strange looks, but the Christmas songs blaring out of the speakers were a lot louder than they had been an hour ago. Lucy hoped it had been loud enough to cover the cacophony of supposed sound Frederika had encouraged her to make, which to Lucy had sounded like a broken violin through a guitar amp being hit by a baseball bat.

'I'll throw in an extra marshmallow,' Ellie said, patting Lucy on the arm. 'I suspect you'll need it.'

'Thanks,' Lucy muttered.

Outside, Tarquin was standing with Rod and Joe.

All three now wore Santa jackets over their overalls as a chill wind rattled in off the sea.

'Was that you singing in there?' Tarquin asked. 'I thought it sounded quite fetching.'

'Frederika wants me to take part in their theatre performance on Christmas Eve,' Lucy said. 'She's out of her mind.'

Tarquin grinned. 'Oh, lovely, don't be so skeptical. It's just a bit of fun, isn't it?'

'Fun if you're not the one being humiliated,' Lucy said. 'She heard me laugh and seemed to think it was because I have some magical vocal ability which is not being properly freed.'

'I heard her voice,' Tarquin said. 'It made the sequins on my t-shirt rattle. If anyone knows, it's her.'

Lucy shrugged. 'Maybe.'

Tarquin waved as Rod and Joe announced they were heading to The Lighthouse for an afternoon pint. Then, turning to Lucy, he said, 'The balloon crew was looking for volunteers for a test. Are you interested?'

'Um, what balloon crew?'

'Come with me.'

Tarquin led Lucy across the ground and behind the stage. There, to her utter amazement, she found a hot air balloon partially inflated, tethered to the rear axle of the lorry she had seen Ellie directing earlier.

Tarquin introduced the two people apparently in charge of it as Dominic and Rebecca. Dominic had a thick sailor's beard flecked with grey and spoke with a Manchester accent as he introduced himself. Rebecca had frizzy ginger hair tied into two buns which looked like radioactive flying saucers trying to lift her off into space. Both wore jackets with Bodmin Balloon Club logos on the back.

'I've found you a volunteer,' Tarquin said, patting Lucy on the back. 'Although I'd be a willing participant too.'

'Sure,' Dominic said. 'Climb on into the basket and we'll warm the old girl up.'

'I've never been in a hot air balloon before,' Lucy whined. 'Are you sure it's safe?'

Rebecca smiled and patted her on the arm. 'That's what we're trying to gauge. We need to send someone up while we measure the effect of the wind off the sea from down here. Don't worry, we won't put it up too high.'

'I'm not sure about this,' Lucy said, but Tarquin had already taken her hand and was pulling her inside. She grimaced as she climbed into a wicker basket that only just came up to her waist.

'Don't move about too much in there,' Dominic said, starting up a gas burner above the basket to fill the listing balloon with hot air. 'We'll only send it up a little way, just to see what happens.'

Lucy was sweating, despite the cold. She glared at Tarquin, who seemed to be enjoying himself.

'Are you sure you know what you're doing?' she said, as the balloon rose above them and she felt a tug on the basket as it strained to lift off.

Tarquin reached into his pocket and pulled out a card. MEMBER, it read. BODMIN BALLOON

CLUB. He grinned. 'Don't worry, I'm a professional.'

'Feeding out now,' Dominic shouted, as Rebecca tugged on a hair-bun with one hand and waved with the other.

The balloon began to rise. In moments Lucy was looking down at the cricket ground like Alice at the White Rabbit's house as she expanded to fill it. Everything seemed so tiny. She could see farther, too, first the rugged fields beyond the cricket ground, then the slope of the clifftop as it turned to couch grass, gorse and bracken, then finally the sea itself, battering against hidden cliffs.

'Wow, we're way higher than thirty feet,' Tarquin said, reaching up to work the burner over their heads. As his fingers adjusted the controls, the burner let out puffs of flame, the balloon shuddering with each one. 'Look, you can see Dad's shop. And over there is where you're staying.'

Lucy turned. Tarquin was right. She could see the holiday park in the valley inland of the village. Theresa's cottage was on one side, with the wooden platforms lined out in orderly formation, each topped with a tent of one kind or another. She spotted hers near to the farmhouse, and could even see a group of tiny people sitting at the tables outside.

'Looks like Mum and Dad are having a good time,' she said.

Tarquin narrowed his eyes. 'I do believe they're playing Twister,' he said, laughing. 'Unless of course I'm getting flares in my eyes from this burner.'

Lucy stared at the tiny group. Tarquin was right. They had moved the picnic tables down onto the grass and had lain a sheet of coloured circles down on the veranda. While Lucy couldn't see who was winning, she hoped they were having a good time.

'Isn't it all so small,' Tarquin said. 'And doesn't it make you think?'

Lucy nodded. Everything seemed so insignificant. Her problems felt overblown beneath the weight of such understanding, and she made a mental note to try better to just go with the flow of things.

'Oh, is that Dan? Um, perhaps not.'

'Where?'

'No, I don't think it's him.'

Lucy followed the line of the high street toward the fudge shop, and saw where Tarquin had been looking. Outside the Castle Hotel at the far end stood two people. One was clearly a woman from the angle of her body, while the other wore a splash of brown which could have been an apron.

They were hugging.

Lucy turned as the burner suddenly cut out. Tarquin was holding onto the control with a grim expression on his face. With a deflated sigh, the balloon slowly began to descend.

'I think we've seen enough for one day,' he said.

22

BEACH BARBEQUE

Lucy tried not to think too hard as she headed back to the holiday park. It had been an interesting day, certainly one of contrasts. She had made some new friends, had a couple of new experiences, but despite everything she felt as deflated as the balloon had been by the time Dominic and Rebecca, apparently satisfied with their test flight, had packed it up again for the night.

As she walked, a cold wind blowing in off the sea to force her hands into her pockets, she didn't want to think about what she had seen from high up in the balloon's basket. What business of hers was it anyway, if Dan was rekindling his love for an old flame? She'd only known him for a couple of days and there was hardly evidence of a spark between them. If anything, she was surprised he hadn't run the other way after her relentless chain of embarrassing gaffes. And even if he did like her, how could she ever compete against a social media monster like Elizabeth Trevellian, so rich she had staff who followed her everywhere, so gorgeous she left cracks in the pavement wherever she went from the jaws of unsuspecting gapers hitting the ground.

There was no comparison. Elizabeth—for all her personality defects—was hot property, and about as unsinkable as Lucy's famous namesake.

It was a no-win situation. Better just to ride it out, do her best to enjoy herself, then make sure that not under any circumstances did she end up down here again next Christmas.

When she got back to the tent, Alan and Valerie were sitting together on the sofa, drinking hot chocolate and watching *The Polar Express* on TV. With a large sigh, Lucy sat down beside them.

'Hi, love, how was your day? We were wondering where you'd got to,' Alan said.

'I was helping out up at the cricket ground,' Lucy said. 'At least I think I was helping.'

'That's great. Have you made any new friends?'

'Dad, I'm not sixteen.'

'I know that, Frances, but … have you made any new friends?'

'I suppose so.'

'That's great. We've been doing our best, too. Oh, is it six o'clock already? Val, we'd better get our walking shoes on. Jen and Mick will be here any minute.'

As if on cue, a sharp zipping sound from nearby was followed by shuffling feet on the terrace outside. A sing-songy voice called, 'Coo-ee! Good evening, happy campers! Is anyone in there?'

Lucy looked around. 'What's going on?'

Valerie gave her a sheepish grin. 'Beach barbeque. Do you want to come?'

'But it's December!'

'So? Apparently there's a decent sheltered spot down at the foot of the castle where we won't all freeze to death. We were told to wrap up warm, though.'

Alan held up a bag. 'Sausages,' he said with a proud grin. 'And not a minute of guilt, either. It's quite a hike back up the hill, apparently.'

Lucy had barely had time to gather her thoughts, but found herself reaching for her jacket. The options were find out what on earth was going on, or sit around and mope. Be positive, she reminded herself.

'Come on!' called Mick. 'The bus will be waiting.'

'I thought you said it was a hike?' Lucy said, turning to Alan with a frown.

He shrugged. 'I meant from the beach up to the car park.'

'Dad!'

'What? I'll only have a couple. Look, I've been told to bulk up. Doctor's orders.'

Lucy glanced at her mother and rolled her eyes. Valerie just laughed. 'Shoes on,' she said.

They walked up to the high street with Mick and Jen, as well as a few other people also heading the same way. Lucy was alarmed to find Frederika at the wheel of the bus waiting just beyond the cattle grid. As Lucy climbed on, the towering Swiss gave her a high-five that sent shudders through Lucy's arm, then boomed, 'Don't be late for practice tomorrow,' loud enough to make the driver's side window give a little rattle.

'Friend of yours?' Alan asked.

'Kind of,' Lucy said, squeezing into a seat behind her parents and lowering her eyes, not wanting to elaborate.

'I love the way this thing is so multi-cultural,' Valerie said. 'It's like going on holiday for Christmas but staying at home at the same time.'

Frederika's bus stopped at another campsite, then once more at the Castle Hotel. To Lucy's dismay, Elizabeth Trevellian climbed on, followed by her crew, Shawn and Peter. Elizabeth planted her hands on her hips, then turned and said something to Peter. With a frustrated grimace, he squeezed past her, then leaned down and asked a man sitting on his own to move into an adjacent seat next to an older lady. With a look of surprise, the man shrugged and agreed. As soon as he had moved, Peter moved aside to allow Elizabeth to sit down. She took a seat, the scent of her perfume making the passengers behind her cringe. Shawn and Peter continued standing as the bus pulled away.

'Who's the princess?' Alan said, loud enough to make the people in front of them turn around, even as Lucy hissed at him to be quiet.

'Is that her?' Valerie asked. 'Is that the woman

who slandered you on the internet? You know, I'm tempted to give her a piece of my mind—'

'Mum, leave it! I can fight my own battles.'

'You haven't done a very good job of it so far.'

Valerie still looked about to go to war for her daughter's honour, but the bus turned down a steep, narrow road, immediately making any movement impossible. Near the front, Shawn and Peter hung on to the overhead hand-rests as they were jerked back and forth. The village vanished behind them, leaving them encased in a tunnel made of steep hedgerows and overhanging trees, only the bus's headlights cutting through the otherwise impenetrable dark. Branches scraped against the windows and there was a collective "whoop!" every time the bus bounced through a pothole.

Finally, just as Lucy was thinking it couldn't get any worse, they turned around a tight corner and the hedgerows opened out. Two angled cliffs rose on either side and they pulled into a small, sandy car park outside a couple of closed tourist shops. Nearby, a sign gave two directions, one back uphill to Tintagel Castle, the other down to Merlin's Cave.

'We've arrived,' Frederika boomed. 'Enjoy your barbeque. The first bus goes back at half past nine. The last is at eleven thirty, so don't miss it, otherwise you have a long walk.' She sang the word "long" in a pealing operatic tenor. Some passengers shook their heads and others clapped. Lucy, sitting near the back, waited until her parents stood up, by which time

Elizabeth Trevellian and her staff had marched off to a path leading down to the beach.

However, "beach" was a generous word. As they descended a steep, uneven path on to the foreshore in the very shadow of Tintagel Castle, Lucy marveled at the jutting headland, which sheltered a narrow stretch of treacherous rocks upon which savage shore-breakers pounded just a hundred metres or so from where a ring of large stones enclosed a billowing bonfire.

'Where's this cave, then?' Alan said, looking around.

'I'd guess that's it,' Valerie said, pointing through the bonfire's rising flames. 'Oh, how pretty.'

Around a dark cave entrance, a string of fairy lights had been strung up, and as they got closer, Lucy saw lights poking out of the sand inside, illuminating a path through the rock.

'I wonder how far in it goes,' she said.

'All the way,' Valerie answered. At Lucy's alarmed look, she added, 'It comes out on the other side of the headland. A hundred metres. They've timed this event perfectly with the tides, by the look of it, as it's full of water at high tide.'

As Lucy stared, a group of figures emerged from the cave. Her jaw dropped at the sight of Father Christmas, followed by a group of reindeer. Then she noticed the opened cans of Carlsberg they were carrying, and realised they were just people wearing costumes. She watched as they went over to the bonfire and sat down, quickly joining in with the chat that was going on.

She was still staring at them when a hand fell on her shoulder. 'Faux pas!' bellowed Ellie as she slid a rucksack off her shoulder and pulled out three Christmas hats. 'Shameful,' she added, handing one to each. 'Don't you remember the rules?'

Alan unzipped his jacket and pulled it wide to reveal a hideous knitted sweater underneath. A pixilated Father Christmas was dancing with a pixilated reindeer around a pixilated Christmas tree.

'Do I pass?' he asked.

'You certainly do, but I'd expect nothing less of the Extravaganza's sponsor,' Ellie said.

'Go on, show her, Val.'

To Lucy's horror, Valerie pulled off her own jacket to reveal a shiny white sweater decorated with a Christmas tree pattern.

'Pass,' Ellie said. 'Lucy?'

'I forgot,' Lucy said sheepishly.

Ellie patted her on the shoulder. 'You're forgiven. It's Christmas, after all. I expect you at the front for the carol singing, though.'

'Carol singing?'

'Once we're all full.'

And with that, Ellie was off, mingling with the other guests, checking for Christmas spirit.

'Let's eat,' Alan said.

A line of barbeques had been set up on the sand between the bonfire and the cave. Alan handed their donation to one of the designated cooks, who smiled and offered them a choice of what was on offer. Lucy stared at the sight of Rod, Tarquin's mechanic friend, wearing a skintight velvet elf suit as he passed over a thick hamburger and then indicated a condiments table set up nearby.

'Extra lettuce, please, Alan,' Valerie instructed, patting him on the stomach. 'And go easy on the sauce.'

'It's grilled,' Alan said. 'It's the healthiest way.'

'Just to be on the safe side,' Valerie said. 'You want to make it to your speech, don't you?'

'I'll be fine,' he said, glancing hungrily back at the line of burgers still sizzling on the barbeque.

'Is Tarquin around?' Lucy asked Rod as she took a burger of her own while her parents argued over the sauce table nearby.

'Sorry, he had to work late,' Rod said. 'They've got a couple of lorries coming in later, bringing the rest of the gear for the Christmas market. He might be down afterwards, but I'm not sure. There are a couple of guys over there from the pub, though. If you want, I'll introduce you in a bit.'

'Anything to avoid Elizabeth Trevellian,' Lucy said, giving him a smile.

Rod laughed. 'Yeah, I think that's why Dan's not here, either. I mean, she's pretty and all, but she's so full of hot air it's a wonder she doesn't float away.'

'Dan's not here? I thought they were like … never mind. Sorry, you look busy. I'll go and say hello to those guys myself.'

'Sure. Talk to you later.'

Her parents had hooked up with Mick and Jen and were engaged in a hearty discussion about some board game Lucy had never heard of, so she walked a little way over to the bonfire and sat down on a log positioned as a bench, from where she could feel its warmth as she ate her burger. A couple of people she had seen up at the cricket ground waved and said hello, but while she returned their greetings, Lucy stayed where she was, staring into the flames as she ate her burger.

Dan wasn't here because Elizabeth was here? But, after what she had seen…?

It didn't bear well to dwell on it. She was growing into a fantasy of her own making, dreaming of something that reality couldn't possibly provide. She couldn't even hold a burning stick to Elizabeth, not to mention the inability to laugh without blowing out a room's windows.

'Frances Drake!'

Like a devil swooning out of the night, Elizabeth Trevellian was suddenly there, sitting beside her, all perfume stench and tickly animal fur. Up close she was a monstrosity, her face so makeup-laden Lucy could have peeled it off and sold it on the internet if the thought of finding a jaw-clacking skull with glowing red eyes beneath hadn't filled her with dread. Elizabeth's teeth gleamed like piano keys and her breath smelled of spearmint. Lucy flinched back, unwittingly letting out a belch as the half a hamburger she had already eaten shifted in her stomach. With her mouth full of another bite, she could only grimace as Shawn lifted his camera.

'Say cheesecake,' Elizabeth said, cocking her head so that her hair got into Lucy's eyes. Lucy flinched again, her mouth half open as the flash filled her vision. By the time it had cleared, Elizabeth had gone, vanished like a genie into smoke.

Lucy coughed, spitting a mouthful of hamburger into the fire, then twisted around. She spotted Elizabeth, together with her photographers, heading for the shoreline. Lucy could only form an ineffectual scowl at the woman's back.

23

FINAL PREPARATIONS

'WHERE DID YOU GET TO LAST NIGHT?' VALERIE said as Lucy sheepishly pulled back her bedroom's curtain and stepped into the little living area where her parents were drinking coffee and eating toast. 'We went through the cave just for a little look and when we came back you'd vanished. If it hadn't been for your text message I might have thought you drowned.'

'I wasn't feeling the holiday spirit,' Lucy said. 'I decided to walk home.'

'Wasn't it dark?'

'Yeah, but there's only one road, and it wasn't that far.'

'What happened? Was it that heinous woman?'

'What woman?'

'Oh, Lucy, don't give me that. You know. I saw her talking to you, and when I got back I checked her Instagram account.'

'You didn't—'

Valerie gave a grim smile. 'I had to change my password—it's scienceislife1, just in case I die—but I wanted to see what she had been posting.'

Lucy sat down next to Alan, who was watching the Spotlight weather news. 'I don't want to think about it.'

'You know what she posted, don't you?'

Lucy gave a despondent nod. The picture was a brutal shot of a pristine Elizabeth draped over a far less photogenic Lucy, one eye half closed as though it was jippy and a piece of hamburger visible through her partially open mouth. The caption read: *I found her again! The barking girl! Could this be the truth behind the Beast of Bodmin Moor myth, or is she just a crazy local? Guesses in the comments below.*

'She's getting a piece of my mind when I next see her,' Valerie said. 'No one humiliates my little girl like that.'

Alan glanced back. 'Don't mess with your mother,' he said. 'She'll make that woman wish she was never born. I've wished I was never born a couple of times, haven't I, love? Like that time I spilt coffee over your new work uniform?'

'Don't bring that up again,' Valerie growled, snapping at the end of the sentence like a dog with a short fuse.

'See what I mean?' Alan said.

Lucy sighed. 'Just leave it. I'm not a teenager. And I don't remember you sticking up for me much back then.'

'As a teenager you have to fight your own battles,'

Valerie said. 'It's character-building. Studies have shown that children with overbearing parents end up in lower-paid professions to those who have a sense of internal motivation developed by a hands-off approach.'

'I'm not exactly raking it in,' Lucy said, taking a piece of toast her mother held out. 'There are three other travel agents on the same street, so commission isn't exactly lying around like used notes in bags.'

'You chose a profession which rewards hard work,' Valerie said. 'That's what I'm talking about.'

'And has really good travel discounts for staff,' Lucy answered. 'What's the plan for today, anyway?'

'We have to be up at the cricket ground by ten o'clock,' Alan said. 'In time for the official opening ceremony.' He grinned, puffing his chest out like a proud rooster. 'As the main sponsor, I have to make a speech.'

'A proud moment for sure,' Valerie said, giving Alan a wink. 'Probably the proudest since you opened that Indian takeaway on Fishponds Road.'

'Half price curry for a year,' Alan said with a sigh. 'Worth every penny, and his carpets still looked great last time we were in there, as I would have expected for such quality.'

'What's after that?' Lucy asked.

'The first official sponsored event. A children's snowman-chain-making competition sponsored by Drake's Carpets. A free lounge carpet to the family of the winner, and every participant gets a free toilet mat.'

'I bet thousands will show up,' Lucy said, unable to avoid a smile.

'Are you going to come?'

'Wouldn't miss it for the world.'

~

Tintagel had transformed overnight. When Lucy had walked back through the village at a little after ten p.m., it had been a hive of activity, with food and trinket stalls being set up all along the road from the Castle Hotel right up to the cricket ground nearly a mile away. What had then been indistinguishable wooden sheds had now taken on an identity with colourful signs outside, and strings of fairy lights hanging right the way along both sides of the street. Lucy saw signs advertising crepes, ice cream, fudge, pasties, German candies, Swedish meatballs, hotdogs, burgers, hot mulled wine, Black Forest gateau, as well as a dozen others selling homemade toys, gifts, and Christmas ornaments. Decorated fir trees in pots lined the road between each stall and the road itself had been closed to traffic, the only exception, according to an information board, being the shuttle buses which would operate at select times during the day.

'They've certainly done a good job,' Valerie said, then leaned forward and tapped the Drake's Carpets logo in the nearest sign's top right-hand corner before giving Alan's hand a squeeze. 'I didn't expect this would be your thing,' she added.

Alan beamed. 'I loved Christmas when I was a

kid, absolutely loved it. And when a circular showed up in the office post asking for sponsors, it just felt right. You know when you just have a feeling about something?'

'A pity there's no snow,' Lucy said. 'Wind and rain don't have the same appeal as a decent blanket of white.'

'Ah, I was just checking this morning,' Alan said. 'It's the twenty-third today. It's going to dump tomorrow night and snow all night, so Christmas Day should be spectacular.'

Lucy glanced up at a crystal clear sky. 'Doesn't look like it at the moment.'

'Weather can change with the click of your fingers here in Cornwall,' Alan said.

'That's why I can't trust what the weather reports say.'

Alan rolled his eyes. 'Oh, I don't listen to them. They said wind and rain. It's Ellie I listen to.'

'Ellie?'

'She's a professional,' Alan said. 'If she says it's going to snow, it'll snow.'

Valerie patted him on the arm. 'I trust you,' she said.

Lucy was skeptical, but after nightfall the village would look spectacular even if it didn't snow. As long as the rain held off and the wind wasn't too strong … everything would be fine. She shivered inside her coat. It was certainly cold enough to snow. If only a few clouds would appear, it might be possible.

They headed for the cricket ground. It, too, had

been completely transformed overnight. What had been a work-in-progress was now a complete festival set-up, with a stage in the middle, a series of food, drinks, and gift stands along one edge, and a number of small fairground rides and attractions for kids filling the space between the stage and the boundary hedge. A marquee filled with tables and chairs, along with the cricket pavilion, were cover in the event of bad weather, but there was also a Christmas-themed merry-go-round, a bouncy castle in the shape of a snowman, and there, near the back of the cricket ground, behind a fenced up area….

Lucy stared. 'Dad, are those reindeer?'

'Sleigh rides,' Ellie said, coming up beside them. 'They start from lunchtime today. We've got eight reindeer, ferried in from Lapland itself. The sleigh is a six-seater, and the route will go down to the end of the high street and back.'

'But there's no snow,' Valerie said.

'Ah, don't worry about that. We have two sets of interchangeable runners. One set has wheels, perfectly adequate for grass or roads. And when the snow comes, we'll switch them out for the sled runners.'

'When it comes?' Valerie said, glancing up.

'Trust me,' Ellie said. She spread her arms. 'How could it not snow at an event like this?'

As she smiled, Lucy caught a little twinkle in her eye, and for a moment wondered if Ellie might not be some kind of Christmas-loving fairy godmother.

'It hasn't snowed in Tintagel between Christmas and New Year for more than thirty years,' Valerie said. 'I checked the historical records. Even then it was barely a dusting.' She smiled. 'However, that's my view as a scientist. As a believer in Christmas … I agree. How could it not?'

'That's right,' Ellie said. 'Just have a little faith.' She clapped her hands together. 'Are you ready for this thing to kick off?'

Alan grinned. 'I feel like I've been waiting for it my whole life.'

A metal barrier had been erected across the entrance to the cricket ground, but Ellie led them through. Already a few groups of people were waiting in the car park, and Lucy glanced back to see a couple of the minibuses pulling in. Through the windscreen of one, Frederika gave her a wave, and then made a numerical symbol with her hands.

Eleven o'clock. Don't be late.

The stage looked far bigger now the set-up was all finished than it had when there were tractors and lorries milling around. Lucy couldn't imagine standing up there in front of hundreds of people making a noise she had never even tried until yesterday. She would definitely need some mulled wine to get her through it.

'You're third on,' Ellie said to Alan as they climbed up onto the stage. Ellie led them to the podium and indicated the microphone stand. 'Just make sure it's on, in case the previous person turned it off. This little button here.'

Alan had gone red-faced. 'Um, okay, sure. How many people will I be speaking to?'

'Well, we're still half an hour from the start. Probably a couple of thousand.' At his horrified expression, she patted him on the arm. 'Don't worry about it. It's all just a bit of fun. Don't forget your Christmas hat.'

Alan reached into his pocket and pulled it out. 'Ready,' he said.

'That's all you need. Come on, let's grab a hot chocolate in the pavilion. We'll put a little bit of brandy in it to calm your nerves.'

They headed inside. A group of people were milling around, talking in nervous tones. Ellie moved through the crowd, scolding people who weren't wearing their Christmas hats, laughing and joking with others, lightening nervous moods. She introduced Alan, Valerie, and Lucy to Donald Tremaine, the official town crier of Truro, the Cornish capital, who was scheduled to open the events. Valerie blended into the crowd, talking easily with people, while Lucy hung by Alan's side, aware he was getting increasingly nervous.

'You'll be fine, Dad,' she told him as Ellie stood up on a chair and called for attention. 'You'll do great.'

'Okay, everyone,' Ellie called as a hush descended on the room. 'It's almost time for the big opening ceremony, and as event coordinator, I'd just like to say something.' She grinned, then clapped her hands together. 'Everyone in this room was involved in some way, in preparation, planning, finance, maintenance, safety … and you've done a stunning job. What I see out there is not Tintagel, a little Cornish village. I see

Tintagel, the Christmas Capital of England! Well done, everyone! This is an event which will be remembered forever, or at least until next year when it'll be eclipsed by something even bigger! Are you ready?'

A great cheer went up from the crowd.

'Then let's get this thing underway!'

24

SPEECHES

A LINE OF STEWARDS ALL DRESSED AS ELVES OPENED the main gates to allow the crowd to enter. It looked like at least five hundred people had been waiting, and a second line of stewards directed them to the stage front area in the middle of the cricket ground. Waiting in a staff area alongside, Lucy watched Ellie jog across to the podium, check the microphone stand and then give it a brief tap before jogging off the other side. From the shadows behind a stage curtain, she gave a thumbs-up to the people waiting on the other side.

To claps and cheers, Donald Tremaine walked out, dressed in full traditional town criers' garb but with a string of tinsel hung around his neck. He leaned over the microphone, spread his arms wide, and hollered, 'It's Chrissssssssmassssss!' in a yodeling version of Slade's famous hit song. The crowd cheered. Donald waited for the applause to die down and then said, 'I'd like to declare the Tintagel Christmas Extravaganza officially open! Christmas joy and happiness to all!'

More cheers came as Donald walked off, his place taken by Denzil Porthleven, who pulled a piece of paper from his pocket.

'Welcome, everyone,' he said, then briefly introduced himself. 'When you think of winter and Cornwall, what do you think of? Closed pasty shops? Rain? Rough seas and empty car parks? Strong winds, mud, cold? From this day onward, I'd like you to associate Cornwall with Christmas. A very special Christmas in a very special part of the world, one made possible by the planning of a small group of talented people, and the hard work of a large group of equally talented people. Passion, drive, and overall a love for fun and entertainment is behind this. I'd like to thank a few people now. Firstly, the people of Tintagel, for not hibernating this year as is the custom and instead opening up all their businesses and organisations and putting up with heaven knows how much noise over the last few days. I'd like to give a special thanks to Ellie, our coordinator all the way from Scotland, and to young Tarquin Bale, who first raised the question over whether this could be done at a parish council meeting last June.'

Lucy lifted an eyebrow. This had all been Tarquin's idea? She was surprised he hadn't said.

Up on the stage, Denzil was reeling off a long list of thanks to all the companies who had volunteered services or expertise. 'And finally, I'd like to invite up

to the stage Mr. Alan Drake of Drake's Carpets of
Bristol, who is this inaugural event's main sponsor.
Alan, if you please.'

'Go on, Dad,' Lucy whispered, patting Alan on
the back as he wiped sweat off his forehead and
climbed up the steps to the stage. He glanced back
and gave them a thumbs-up, although his face was
ashen and he looked beyond terrified.

'Will he be all right?' Lucy asked Valerie, standing
beside her.

'I'm sure he'll be fine,' her mother said. 'Oh, wait
a minute—'

Halfway across to the stage, Alan had begun
fumbling in his pocket with increasing freneticism.
Eventually he pulled the lining out into a neat
triangle, but nothing came out with it. His eyes
widened and he glared at the floor as though a mouth
had just appeared to swallow up something
important.

'He's realised his speech is missing,' Valerie said,
putting a hand over her eyes. 'This could be
interesting … or perhaps traumatic.'

'Mum, what did you do?' Lucy whispered.

'Don't worry. Just listen.'

Alan reached the microphone and cleared his
throat. He glanced back at Lucy and Valerie,
mouthing something about looking on the floor. Lucy
glanced down, but there was no sign of a piece of
paper. She looked back up and shook her head.

'Just wing it!' Valerie hissed.

Alan, after another moment of indecision and an

increasingly fraught look from Denzil, turned to the microphone.

'Um, welcome,' he said. 'I, um, lost my speech.' Cheers rose from the crowd. A few people pumped fists into the air. 'Merry Christmas.' More cheers. 'Um, well … when I was a child, I really loved Christmas,' Alan began, holding the microphone in two hands like the end of a rope thrown to a drowning man. 'I was around fourteen when I finally figured out that Father Christmas wasn't real—' some cheers, a few jeers, and a lot of laughter '—and it was never quite the same.' When my daughter, Frances—' a few shouts of 'Frances Drake!' and some more laughter, which made Lucy close her eyes and grimace '—was little, me and her mother, Valeria—'

Lucy frowned. 'Is that your real name, Mum? And people rip on me for sounding historical.'

Valerie scowled. 'Let's just say no more about it, shall we?'

'—tried to give her the best Christmas possible, but eventually she grew up, too. Christmas lost its magic for her as well, and she stopped even coming home.'

The crowd booed. Valerie gave Lucy a supportive pat on the arm. 'Don't worry, he'll stop in a minute. He's right off script. None of this was in his original speech. Just wait it out.'

'My father built up Drake's Carpets and passed it on to me when he was too frail to continue. He loved that business, and he was even more proud that we remained independent, that we didn't sell ourselves out to some multinational corporation. Drake's Carpets has always prided itself on importing carpets that were unavailable elsewhere, as well as offering expert advice and a fitting service that no national chain store could match.'

Out in the crowd, some people had begun to look at their watches. Valerie glanced at Lucy and shrugged. 'He's back on script now. Boring, isn't it? I hid that speech for a good reason.'

'Mum, you didn't—'

'Studies have shown that the best part of a man's character comes out when he's under pressure,' Valerie said with a smile.

'I'd really like to see some of these studies sometime.'

Valerie winked. 'They're classified.'

'I lived for my business, and my business lived through me,' Alan droned on as the crowd began to get restless. 'But do you know what the best times were?'

A few people shouted, 'Closing time?' Someone else added, 'The pub after work?'

'Uh oh, he's deviating again,' Valerie said.

'Can't we make him stop?' Lucy said. 'I'm not sure how much more I can take, and I think the crowd might riot if we don't shut him up.'

Valerie gave her a reassuring pat on the arm. 'Let him have his moment,' she said.

Alan was looking out at the crowd, letting the dramatic pause linger on and on. Finally he nodded. 'Those days when we were quiet, when no one came in. I would take off my glasses, tie a rag around my head, and climb up on to a mound of rugs. I would become a pirate. The chairs became sharks, and other mounds of rugs were the navy, coming to get me. With a metre-ruler in hand as my cutlass, I would fight them off.' Ripples of laughter shook the crowd. Alan, not even smiling, gave a grim nod. 'That's right. And on other days I would venture among the trees that the great rolls of carpet became, an adventurer, an explorer, hunting dinosaurs in a prehistoric forest. Sometimes I'd come across a caveman hiding there, even though it was just the floor manager, or one of the temp staff skiving off to check his phone, and I would run from them, to hide in a cave beneath a desk.'

People were slapping each other on the back, coughing into their hands. Finally Alan smiled. 'Imagination, friends. That was what it was. Imagination and fun. And what time of the year captures imagination more, and encapsulates fun more, than Christmas?'

People had begun to nod, to mutter with agreement, even to cheer. Lucy felt a sudden bulging in her chest, a lump building on her throat. As her mother, smiling as she wiped a tear from her eye, took Lucy's hand, Lucy recognised it as pride.

'And that's why, when I was given the opportunity to be a sponsor for this first ever Tintagel Christmas Extravaganza, the absolutely last word that was ever going to come to mind was "no". It's my absolute delight to be here, to be a sponsor for this event, and to be part of everything. Thank you everyone, for coming here, and making this event special.'

The crowd cheered. Alan stepped back from the microphone and mouthed at Denzil that he was done. Denzil peered through a curtain at the stage side, and a moment later fireworks rose into the air, their colours making little impact against the bright sky, but shaking everything with their sound. And then, as the cheers had begun to abate, they rose again. Lucy stepped out of the staff area into the edge of the crowd and looked where all the eyes were pointing: at the huge hot air balloon rising behind the stage, its front a mass of flickering fairy lights writing *MERRY CHRISTMAS!* across the bulge of its surface.

Alan, his speech over, continued to stand awkwardly in the centre of the stage until Ellie waved him off. Lucy ran to give him a hug, and Valerie a kiss on the cheek. Alan beamed. Denzil Porthleven patted him on the shoulder and then Ellie was waving them through a curtain into the backstage area, calling out, 'Staff hot chocolates are ready!'

Lucy waited for a moment, watching the air balloon, and was just about to join them when a familiar voice beside her said, 'Your dad made a great speech.'

Lucy felt a prickle of nerves as she turned to find Dan standing beside her, looking up at the hot air balloon with a smile on his face.

25

KRAMPUS

'Um, thanks,' she said, feeling her ability to maintain rational thought abruptly leave her. 'That's nice of you to say.'

'I heard you were down at the beach barbeque yesterday,' Dan said. 'I'm afraid I didn't get to go down. I was busy helping Dad set up the stall for the Christmas Market.'

Lucy shrugged. 'I went for a bit,' she said. 'It was a bit … cold, um, so I came back up.'

Dan nodded. 'You've been lucky so far,' he said. 'The winds can be brutal when they really get going. I'm worried we'll get a gale come in off the sea and ruin Christmas for everyone.'

'I suppose it's a risk,' Lucy said, wondering why, of all things, they were talking about the weather. Part of her was afraid to ask about how Dan had known she had attended the beach barbeque, in case he followed Elizabeth's social media. It was possible one of Tarquin's friends had told him, but it was just as possible that he had seen Elizabeth's photo comparing her to the Beast of Bodmin Moor.

'How long are you here?' Dan asked.

'Um, I'm not sure yet. I don't have to work again until the third.'

'So you might stay right through New Year?'

Lucy shrugged. 'Maybe.' Was that a hint of excitement in his voice, or was he just being friendly? She reminded herself that—on the off chance that he actually liked her—his dental practice was only a short way from where she worked in Bristol.

'Well, if you've got some free time—'

'Lucy, quick, I need your help!'

She turned. Her mother was peering through the curtain into the backstage area, holding it up with one hand and waving at her with the other. Lucy suppressed a groan. Why now, of all times?

'You'd better go,' Dan said. He lifted a hand and gave her a light touch on the shoulder. Lucy closed her eyes, wanting to shut out the world, but it was gone almost as soon as it had been there. 'I'll catch up with you later.'

He was gone without any further goodbyes. Valerie was still waving at her, eyes wide as though waiting for Lucy's decision. Reluctantly Lucy hurried over.

'I really hope there's been some big disaster,' Lucy said, glaring at her mother.

'Your dad needs someone to help him carry a box of stationery over to the marquee,' Valerie said.

'Is that it?'

Valerie smiled. 'It's an important job, and he wants you to help him judge the paper-chain competition as well. Plus, I could see you were getting nervous.'

'*What?*'

'Got to keep them keen,' Valerie said, smiling. 'Make them work a bit.'

'What are you talking about?'

'That young man. Dan, isn't it? He was giving you a right looking over.'

'No, he wasn't!'

Valerie shrugged. 'If you say so. Come on, help your father, please. I'm worried he's going to have a coronary.'

Cheeks burning, but still feeling obsessively intrigued with what her mother had said, Lucy grabbed a box of scissors and hurried after her father, who was huffing his way through the milling customers with a box of old Christmas cards and paper in his hands.

Inside the marquee, Tarquin had taken charge of a group of thirty children waiting to make paper chains. Alan and Lucy set their boxes down, and then with a clap of his hands, Tarquin made a short opening speech. A couple of minutes later, the children were rushing for the boxes, retrieving materials, and taking their finds back to a line of chairs and desks set up inside a square made by four portable paraffin heaters. While Alan walked up and down the lines, muttering encouragement to the industrious children, Lucy wandered over to Dan's brother.

'Are you having a good time?' he said.

Lucy shrugged. 'I'm trying.'

'That's great. I saw you bumped into Dan.'

Lucy felt a prickle of embarrassment. Everyone here seemed to notice everything else. 'I said hello,' she muttered, giving a shrug. 'That was about it.'

'He's having a hard time,' Tarquin said.

'About what?'

'That meatgrinding witch of an ex-girlfriend of his,' Tarquin said, with sudden vehemence. 'She's as good as stalking him.'

'Why?'

Tarquin shrugged. 'I can't believe she has any interest in him, but she's acting like she wants him back.' He shook his head. 'No chance. I will not allow it.'

Lucy couldn't help a smile at Tarquin's stoicism. 'Does Dan need you to arrange his love life?'

'That heathen witch … if Krampus himself showed up, it couldn't ruin Christmas more.'

'Krampus?'

Tarquin scowled. In his elf costume he looked comical as he clenched his fists and rode up and down on his toes as though his anger might cause him to lift off.

'She was one year above Dan at school,' Tarquin said. 'Dan was the cool kid in his year, the one all the girls liked. He wasn't popular with the boys because he had an openly gay younger brother—' Tarquin

165

poked two thumbs into his chest and grinned, as though Lucy couldn't have guessed '—whom he always stuck up for. That only made the girls swoon, though. There were some nice girls in his year, too, far better than her. She already had a modeling contract and was out of school for weeks at a time on exotic photography trips. She decided she needed to snare Dan before she left. So, of course, she did.'

'What happened?'

'Oh, she played the game, pretended to be in love with him and then dumped him on Christmas Day. He was seventeen, she eighteen. He was distraught. He drank a bottle of vodka and decided to go surfing off Tintagel Head. That's when he got injured.'

'He fell off his board?'

Tarquin shook his head. 'He never made it as far as the water. Fell down the steps from the car park. Broke his left leg and collarbone. He was in hospital most of that Christmas and in casts until the end of January.'

'Sounds painful.'

'Even worse was that at New Year Elizabeth was on the yacht of some famous photographer in Monaco. We saw it in the newspapers.'

'Ouch.'

'It turned out she had been with the guy all along, but pictures of her and Dan together on the cliffs got leaked to the press.' Tarquin pouted, making quotation marks with his fingers. 'The photographs were clever with their angles, made it look like Dan had dumped her. The press was all sympathetic to

Elizabeth, and for the whole Christmas period we had journalists knocking on the door wanting to know Dan's opinions and why he had broken up with someone as perfect as Elizabeth Trevellian. He hadn't even realised she was that famous, because at that time my mother had only been gone a couple of years and we had no time for social media or the internet. We were busy in our free time keeping the fudge shop on its feet.'

'She sounds like a bit of a player.'

Tarquin scowled again. 'Elizabeth Trevellian is a media queen,' he said. 'All she cares about is her position in life. She has no soul, or if she has, it's buried so deep she can no longer find it. She's here for one reason only—to raise her profile. She has no interest in Dan, but she'll hunt him like the last rhino of a species just to get that trophy photograph.'

'What about Dan?'

'He's a gentle giant, but at times he's an idiot. He won't tell her to get lost like he should, because he's too nice. He's always been too nice. He might look like he could pull trees out of the ground, but he's far more likely to dig up little seedlings stuck in the shade and replant them somewhere with a bit more sun. You know, one of the reasons why he qualified as a dentist was to help impoverished children with teeth problems. There's a children's home not far from here, and he used to teach some of them to surf on a weekend when he was younger. Many of them had been neglected by their parents, given nothing but rubbish to eat, and their teeth had suffered. Dentistry gave him a skill that would give something back to those kids, and others like them.'

'It sounds like he has a good heart.'

'Too good, sometimes. Trolls like Elizabeth Trevellian have no problem taking advantage of him.'

'But he definitely doesn't like her?'

'Not at all.'

'But ... we saw them hugging.'

Tarquin grimaced. 'I'm sure it wasn't what it looked like.' He gave a frenetic shake of the head. 'Absolutely not. No ... way.'

26

GOODBYES

THE WINNING PAPER-CHAIN WAS NEARLY THIRTY feet of taped-together recycled Christmas cards cut into an alternating Father Christmas, sleigh, and reindeer pattern. The boy's parents were delighted with the idea of a new living room carpet, ordered and fitted on request, and the boy himself was delighted to receive a box of assorted Christmas goodies. All the other participating kids, as well as receiving a Christmas-patterned toilet mat, got a consolation prize of a chocolate reindeer with Smarties inside. Exhausted after judging the event, Lucy and Alan headed back to the cricket pavilion, recommissioned as the staff quarters. As they passed the main stage, Lucy paused to watch a group of primary school children doing a cute choreographed dance to *Santa Claus is Coming to Town* while a crowd of a couple of hundred watched with delight as they clapped along.

In the pavilion, the off-duty staff members were gathered around a table, drinking hot chocolate. 'Coming through!' came a shout from through a door behind the bar which led into a small kitchen. Ellie appeared, carrying a metal tray, almost too wide for her arms to stretch. She ran to the table and dropped it down seemingly moments before it sent her sprawling. The group cheered at the sight of a couple of hundred steaming mince pies.

'Denzil's bringing the plates,' Ellie gasped. 'And no one touches anything until the clotted cream arrives.'

Soon everyone was tucking in to fresh mince pies with local clotted cream. Lucy patted her stomach, unable to ignore a glow of happiness. Freshly baked, the mince pies tasted spectacular. They had a hint of spice to them which Lucy had never tasted in shop-bought ones.

Ellie sauntered over as Alan, Valerie, and Lucy finished up. 'Great job with the paper-chain competition,' she said. 'You're all good with your roles from now on, aren't you?'

Alan gave her a salute. 'Got it.'

Ellie smiled and let out a contented sigh. 'Then my work here is done.'

'You're really leaving?' Valerie asked.

Ellie smiled. 'My son's getting married on Christmas Day. I have to get back to Scotland. I'm catching a lunchtime train and flying up to Edinburgh from London.'

'We'll miss you,' Alan said. 'You've done an amazing job.'

'It was a group effort,' Ellie said. 'Everyone played their part, and it's not over yet. I want you to promise me that you'll do everything you can to enjoy yourselves and make sure everyone has a great time.'

'We promise,' Alan and Valerie said together.

'Good.' Ellie turned to Lucy. 'Frederika has kindly offered to give me a lift down to Bodmin Parkway. She thought you might want to come. It'll be a good chance for you to practice for your performance tomorrow night.'

Alan and Valerie looked amused, but Lucy forced herself to shrug off the nerves she felt and gave Ellie a wide smile. 'That's a great idea,' she said, then added, 'Although I don't think I'll need much practice.'

Ellie's bags were already loaded onto Frederika's bus. As the huge Swiss pulled out of the car park, Ellie waved through the windows at everyone who had come to see her off. As soon as they were out of the cricket ground and across the high street, taking a road that intersected with the A39 meandering down the Cornish coast, Ellie turned to Lucy and wiped a tear out of her eye.

'I'll miss this place,' she said. 'I know I was only here a couple of days, but I could really feel the spirit. You're going to have a great Christmas.

Unfortunately, I have my own Christmas village to take care of.' She smiled. 'You should visit sometime.'

As they drove down the A39, through Camelford and then turned onto the B3266 to Bodmin, Ellie told Lucy about her son and future daughter-in-law.

'I'd been hoping Henry would settle down for years,' Ellie said. 'He did get married once before but he got that one all wrong. She was a right so-and-so, and it was no surprise when she ran out on him. I brought both my lads up right, you know, to be kind and respectful to people and animals, to treat as you wish to be treated, and all that.' She sighed. 'No matter how nice you are, there's always someone who'll take advantage of you. Some people have no shame, do they?'

Lucy nodded, unable to avoid thinking about Elizabeth Trevellian. She had an urge to check the woman's social media to see how many people were laughing at her comparison to the Beast of Bodmin Moor, but tried to be mature and rise above it. It wasn't easy, though.

'I'm so glad he found someone in the end,' Ellie said. 'Henry and Maggie make such a lovely couple.'

'I hope I get to meet them sometime,' Lucy said.

Ellie smiled. 'Come up and visit any time you like,' she said. 'Although I particularly recommend the Christmas season. That's when my little village is most … magical.'

They pulled in to the bus parking outside Bodmin Parkway railway station. Frederika wished Ellie good luck and stayed with the bus while Lucy helped Ellie with her bags onto the platform.

It was only five minutes to the train. 'Thank you for everything,' Lucy said, giving Ellie another hug.

'Make sure you tell Denzil to get that website updated,' Ellie said. 'I want to see pictures next time I have a look.'

'Will do.'

'And you … just one last thing,' Ellie said, catching Lucy's gaze. 'I want no more moping about or negativity. Be yourself, and don't be afraid to be yourself. Every single one of us is different and very few of us are even a little bit perfect. And those of us who think it are usually the least perfect of all. Being different is what makes us each unique, and when you realise that society is just a great big clash of different forms of uniqueness, it becomes so much more interesting. Revel in who you are, and if other people don't like it … well, bugger them.'

'I'll try to remember that,' Lucy said, as Ellie grinned.

'Well, here's my train. Best of luck, and I look forward to hearing all about it.'

Lucy stepped back as the train pulled in. She helped Ellie with her cases and then waited as Ellie found her seat. Lucy took a deep breath. The guard blew a whistle, and the train began to move. Lucy wiped away a tear as Ellie gave her one last wave before the train took her away.

Frederika was standing outside the bus when Lucy

returned. 'She caught the train, or she missed the train?'

'She caught it.'

'Fantastic. Then we shall return. Are you ready to practice for ze performance tomorrow night?'

Lucy grinned. She looked up at the sky, her eyes widening as a single snowflake drifted down in front of her, landing at her feet, where it dissolved into a tiny droplet of shadow on the car park surface.

'I've never felt readier,' she said.

27

MINCE PIE HUNT

Lucy's throat was aching by the time they got back to Tintagel cricket ground. She found her mother and father inside the pavilion, which had been turned into a kitchen of sorts, with trestle tables laden with trays of freshly baked mince pies and large jugs of frothy eggnog.

'Did Ellie get off all right?' Alan asked.

'No problem,' Lucy croaked. 'It was a shame to see her go, but she said to make sure we all enjoy ourselves.'

'We're working on it,' Valerie said, letting out an exhausted sigh. 'Literally working on it. Your dad volunteered us for the mince pie hunt.'

'The what?'

'It's an event for kids. Kind of like an Easter egg hunt.' She turned to the table. 'See all those? Each one has to be put into one of the coloured pots underneath the table.' Valerie nudged a cardboard box with her foot. Lucy pulled it out and opened the top to reveal a couple of hundred Christmas-decorated boxes, each about the size of her hand.

'Be a love and start filling them up,' Alan said. 'Rod and Joe were supposed to be doing it, but the merry-go-round had a problem with its gearbox so they had to rush off.'

'That was their excuse,' Valerie said, narrowing her eyes. 'It looked to be working fine to me.'

Lucy smiled. 'Sure, I'll get to it.'

Humming along to Christmas songs played on a CD player in a corner, Lucy packed the fresh mince pies into the boxes as her parents brought more, wrapping each in a little piece of tin foil so that it wouldn't spoil or get damaged. After half an hour, she had done a couple of hundred, and her arms were starting to hurt.

'Is that everything?' she asked, as her mother pulled off a pair of plastic gloves and sat down with a tired sigh.

'Great. Alan, what's next?'

Alan, wearing a reindeer-patterned apron spotted with flour and lumps of mincemeat, went to a side door and leaned out.

'Denzil, we're done!'

A moment later the head of the parish council came hurrying in. He wore a Father Christmas puppet on one hand and an elf puppet on the other. A string of fairy lights flashed around his neck and his Christmas hat was askew.

'The kids are getting restless,' he said, grinning.

'Great work. It's two o'clock now, and the hunt starts at three. I'll go and see who I can rope in to help us hide these things.'

He went out, returning a couple of minutes later with ginger-bobbed Rebecca from the balloon team and a huffing Jed Penrose, who had apparently run all the way up from The Lighthouse Keeper, leaving his wife to run the bar.

'Right,' Denzil said. 'Thanks for helping out, everyone. The hunt area is past the field behind the ground, on the cliff area marked by flags. Hide all your pies in that area. Once the game gets underway, we'll be acting as stewards to make sure no one goes too close to the cliff, but each child has to be accompanied by an adult anyway, so we shouldn't have any problems. Any questions?'

Lucy raised a hand. 'What's the eggnog for?'

Denzil grinned. 'Staff and parents after-party. Right, let's hop to it.'

The team headed out. The Christmas Extravaganza was in full swing, with a Christmas hits covers band playing on the main stage, while in the marquee a couple of hundred people were taking part in an Irish line-dancing class. The merry-go-round, which seemed to be working again, was packed with children, while all along the boundary edge, the food stalls were doing a roaring trade as customers strolled up and down, laughing and making merry.

Lucy couldn't help but feel the magic in the air slowly growing. She glanced up at the sky. If only it would snow.

They finished hiding the mince pie boxes among the long grass of the clifftop just ten minutes before the game was due to start. Instructed by Denzil, Lucy took up a stewarding position on the edge of the playing area, just short of the coast path which wound its way through the couch grass. The sea was calm, a chilly but light breeze blowing in off the water. As they waited to begin, Jed Penrose, skirting around the perimeter, came wandering over for a chat.

'Hey, lass,' he said. 'Didn't see you in the pub last night. You coming down this eve?'

Lucy smiled. 'I might. Depends how much energy I have left after all of this.'

''Tis Christmas karaoke night,' Jed said. 'Chrissy songs only. You sing?'

'Sing?'

'Yeah.'

Lucy shrugged. 'Not really.'

'Game on. All for a laugh, ain't it?'

'That's right,' Lucy said, wondering if she could remember the words to anything at all. She had nightmarish memories of karaoke nights during her university days when she had drunk too much and been persuaded to sing, finding the situation funny enough to bellow into the microphone before being politely asked to step down. Perhaps it was another one to give a miss … but she remembered what Ellie had said. She looked up at Jed and smiled.

'I wouldn't miss it for the world,' she said, as

across the grass by a gate in the hedge behind the cricket ground, Denzil clapped his hands together and waved forward a group of eager-faced children.

'On the count of three, I declare the Christmas Mince Pie Hunt open. Are you ready? One ... two ... three!'

The kids rushed into the grass. Lucy grinned as a couple got over-excited and went tumbling over, springing back up as the grass bounced beneath them. A moment later, one of them came upon a cluster of boxes hidden beneath the roots of an exposed bush. Still laughing, the kids scooped them up and carried them back to their parents, who were wading through the grass in pursuit.

A few minutes later, Denzil clapped his hands together. 'Time's up!' he called, waving in the last few children still searching for a couple of elusive boxes. Lucy was about to follow when she looked up and noticed Elizabeth Trevellian walking along the coast path in their direction.

Elizabeth appeared to be alone. As the model, wearing jeans and a white roll-neck sweater, paused, turned to face the sea, and wrapped her arms around herself in a gesture which suggested both vulnerability and loneliness, Lucy couldn't help but hear an imaginary piano line tinkling over the top of the scene, playing a melancholy lament to a woman perhaps yearning for a lover gone off to war. Lucy found herself transfixed, enraptured by Elizabeth, who seemed suddenly stripped of all the baggage that she carried everywhere. She was human after all, and perhaps behind the visage of shallowness, there was a woman with depth and vulnerability.

Lucy took a step forward, her shoe nudging something buried in the grass by her feet. A last mince pie, undiscovered. She picked up the little box and climbed out of the grass onto the path. She looked down at the box in her hands. It was a small thing, little more than a gesture, but it was Christmas, and a time for forgiving. It didn't matter what Elizabeth had done, publicly humiliating Lucy to the amusement of her thousands of social media followers. Lucy could be the one to offer an olive branch, and perhaps they could even be friends.

Lucy had covered half the distance to where Elizabeth stood, one hand holding back the billowing hair from her eyes, a frown on her face, the threat of imminent tears in her eyes, when something shifted in the grass between them. Lucy stopped, fingers clenching over the box.

A reflective mirror, lying flat, with Peter lying beneath it in a little hollow, almost out of Lucy's view. As she stopped, the box held limply out in front of her, she saw Shawn, too, crouched behind a bush a little way off the path, camera clicking incessantly as he captured the full extent of Elizabeth's mock vulnerability.

Lucy had nowhere to hide. She could only stand meekly and wait as Elizabeth turned, the look of anguish on her face turning to one first of shock, then derision, and then finally to amusement.

'The Beast!' she cried, throwing her arms up in

the air. 'Oh, quickly, Shawn, capture it on camera! It could be worth thousands to the Sunday papers! And what's this? You brought me a present? It's intelligent, Shawn! It's intelligent! I think we found the missing link! The scientific community will rejoice for years to come!'

Lucy couldn't even speak. She stared, numb, dumb, stunned, as Elizabeth bounded over, threw an arm around her shoulders and grinned as Shawn clicked away. Peter, behind the game, nearly tripped as he stumbled out of the grass and lay on the ground beneath them, angling his mirror upward to reflect more light onto their faces.

'Oh, thank you,' Elizabeth said, snatching the box out of Lucy's hand. 'What a lovely surprise!' She ripped the top off the box and pulled out the neatly folded envelope of tin foil. She unwrapped it, her mouth going wide as she looked up at Lucy. 'Did you make this yourself? Did you? Oh, how clever. You can cook, too. Just fantastic. Ooh, it smells a little off, but I'm sure the mice will like it.' Elizabeth tossed the mince pie over her shoulder, then threw the box and the tin foil down. 'Thank you so much, Beast. Merry Christmas to you too!'

With that, Elizabeth leaned in and pretended to kiss Lucy on the cheek. Lucy could still say nothing. She stared as Elizabeth bounded off, Shawn and Peter hurrying to catch up. Just before they were out of sight, Peter glanced back and gave Lucy an apologetic shrug, then they were gone, over a rise of the coastal path and out of sight.

Lucy just stared, then slowly she bent down and picked up the rubbish Elizabeth had thrown away, putting the remains of the mince pie back into the little box.

'Krampus,' she muttered, finding her voice at last, giving only a disbelieving shake of her head.

28

HUSTLING FUDGE

THE REST OF THE GROUP HAD ENTIRELY MISSED Lucy's encounter with Elizabeth, having already headed back across the cricket ground. Lucy caught up with them just as they were going into the pavilion.

'Where did you get to?' Alan asked. 'You didn't go for a detour to the crepe stall, did you?'

Lucy sighed. 'I wouldn't dare without you, Dad,' she said.

'That's my girl. Right, staff eggnog. Do you want it non-alcoholic or loaded?'

'How much brandy have you got?' Lucy asked.

Jed Penrose took a plastic bag from under the table and pulled a bottle out of it. Grinning, he said, 'Finest Estonian navy rum. A gift from the lad setting up a European booze stall outside the pub. Now, I'll drop a little of this into the mix on the promise that no one gets too drunk to attend Christmas karaoke at the pub tonight.' He passed it to Denzil, who unscrewed the cap, took a sniff that made him wince, then began topping up the drinks. 'I want a good showing from the locals,' Jed said, 'to show all these foreigners how we party, Tintagel-style.' He patted Lucy on the shoulder. 'You, lass, are an honourary local. I'm looking forward to seeing you with that microphone in your hands.'

'Do you sing?' Valerie asked, taking a glass of eggnog from Denzil as the parish council head began dishing it out.

Lucy shrugged. 'Most people have at some point, haven't they?'

'Well, just choose your song wisely. Your father's found out recently that shower renditions don't transfer well to the stage. Ooh, this is strong, isn't it? Easy on the rum, there, Denzil.'

Lucy laughed as her mother burped. She felt among friends, even though the shock of her encounter with Elizabeth was still fresh in her mind. She took a glass of eggnog offered by Denzil and took a sip.

'Woah,' she muttered. 'That tingles.'

'Lad said they broke these over the bows of the ships,' Jed explained, holding up the bottle, which was now only half full. 'Didn't do much to stop them sink, but if they got into trouble the boys would all suck on a piece of wood to make sure they went down with a smile.'

Everyone laughed. Without realising it, Lucy found herself laughing too. Jed clapped her on the shoulder. 'Fine pair of lungs you've got there, lass,' he said. 'I imagine you're something of a virtuo-see-o.'

Unsure if he meant "virtuoso" or some Cornish equivalent, Lucy just smiled. For the first time in as long as she could remember, she didn't feel the shame of letting her laugh come out in public. Well, maybe just a little. As she looked around, she realised everyone had already moved on to their next topic of conversation, and no one was looking at her.

Perhaps her laugh wasn't as bad as she thought.

Or perhaps it was just the rum.

Alan had volunteered himself and Valerie to help with a communal Christmas dinner for a group of elderly being bussed in that evening from local care homes. Lucy, with some time to herself, went out of the cricket ground and took a stroll down the high street, now beautifully transformed into a stunningly illuminated international Christmas market. At Denzil's offer, she had partaken in a second glass of the potent eggnog, but she wasn't drunk, not at all, as she wandered among the stalls and shops as the sun dipped and fell beneath the sea.

And she certainly wasn't hoping to bump into Dan as she found herself outside the fudge shop, now transformed into a small café with the fudge sold from a stall outside. Mark was there, looking busy in an apron and Christmas hat, but there was no sign of Dan. Instead, Mark was being assisted by a tall, grinning German wearing a pair of plastic reindeer horns.

'Lucy!' Mark called the moment he spotted her. She had been planning to quietly slip on by, perhaps walk to the end of the high street, but not at all because she wanted to find out where Elizabeth Trevellian was and make sure Dan wasn't with her. Not at all. Instead, she found herself waved up to the fudge stall where a huge hand reached out to take hers.

'This is Klaus,' Mark said. 'He's from Frankfurt am Main. Klaus, this is Lucy, a young friend of mine.'

The warmth with which Mark referred to Lucy as a friend doused the fire of her worries with a bucketful of Christmas spirit. She smiled at Klaus, his blonde hair ruffled by the wind around the frame of the reindeer horns, his blue eyes sparkling.

'It is my pleasure to meet you,' Klaus said. 'I hear from Mark that your father is one of the event's sponsors?'

Lucy smiled. 'If you ever want a new carpet, you know where to come,' she said.

'Why don't you stop for some fudge?' Mark said, gesturing to the stall. 'Klaus has shown me a few new recipes. Over here we have dark apple, tiramisu, and cream cherry.'

Lucy started to shake her head, then changed her mind. 'Okay, just a sliver of each,' she said.

'Lucy here is a bit of an expert with fudge,' Mark said. 'I only had to show her once. She's a natural, I tell you.'

'If you have no plan, perhaps you could help us out for a while,' Klaus said. 'Two old men like us don't attract the customers like a pretty face like yours would.'

Lucy blushed. 'I'm not—'

'I have two sons,' Klaus said. 'I'm sure both would be delighted to meet you.'

'I don't—' Lucy shifted awkwardly from foot to foot. Klaus was still grinning, and Mark laughed as he handed Lucy a small bag. 'Klaus is right. I tell you what, if you hang around here for an hour, I'll make sure there's a couple of drinks for you down The Lighthouse tonight.'

'Well, I'm not really doing much.' *Other than trying to spy on Elizabeth Trevellian*, Lucy didn't say.

'Great.' Mark handed Lucy an apron and a glass of mulled wine. 'Come on, let's hustle them a little. It's Christmas, after all.' He stepped out from behind the stall and walked down to the street. 'Finest fudge!' he called as people ambled by. 'The only Christmas-spiced flavours in the whole of North Cornwall!'

His enthusiasm was infectious. A few minutes later, Lucy was standing beside him, imploring passersby to try samples from a tray of small pieces Klaus had cut up. A line of people had formed, and as the snowball effect brought more people wanting to get their hands on Mark and Klaus's unique flavours, the two men struggled to keep up with the demand. Lucy, sipping from a glass of mulled wine, aware her cheeks must be glowing as the Christmas hat flopped across her face, hadn't realised selling fudge could be so much fun.

Before she knew it, she was laughing freely along with the local people as they oohed and aahed at the delicious flavours. Mark had cooked up a small batch of chili-flavoured fudge earlier in the day, and Lucy was offering a form of roulette off a wide platter. Customers chose a piece of fudge at random, and anyone who showed the obvious discomfort of finding the chili flavour won a small bag of confectionery. Soon, the little fudge stand was one of the busiest on the street. Mark had even sold a few t-shirts with the company logo on them.

After an hour or so, Mark came down to where Lucy was still standing on the street, holding out her platter of remaining samples.

'Brilliant,' he told her. 'I think you deserve a break. One of my lads just showed up, wondering if I could spare you for a bite to eat. It's dinner time, don't you know.'

Lucy spun around, her heart thumping as she prayed it would be Dan, but instead found Tarquin standing beside the fudge, an illuminating Father Christmas flickering on a sweater that at any other time of the year would have warranted an emergency call to the fashion police. He lifted a hand and gave her a little wave.

What disappointment she had felt swiftly faded at the smile on Tarquin's face. He skipped across to her and took the platter out of her hands. 'I apologise for my father's shameless taking advantage of you,' he said. 'I overheard a couple of people talking about the nice girl with the fantastic laugh who was selling fudge, and I came down here to save you.'

'Fantastic laugh?'

Tarquin lifted an eyebrow. 'See? You didn't even notice, did you?'

Lucy frowned. He was right. She had been laughing along with the customers as they tried their luck at finding the chili fudge, and not once had she felt embarrassed or ashamed. Her laugh hadn't even seemed that bad.

'I don't know what happened,' she said.

'You relaxed. And now that you're relaxed, I'd like to invite you to experience the pleasure of my company for a slap-up dinner at the best place in town.' He grinned. 'The best *plaice*.'

Lucy smiled. 'Sure,' she said. 'Why not?'

29

SOCIAL JUSTICE

TARQUIN WAS SO CHARMING AND FUNNY THAT HAD he been a bit more masculine Lucy would have felt disappointed he was gay. The finest restaurant in the village, down a little side street just past the cricket ground, turned out to be just as he had implied, an up-market fish n' chips shop which wouldn't be seen dead doing takeaways. Catering for wealthier older customers, it had a pretty olde worlde charm with candelabras on the walls and pretty alcoves containing Medieval-style tapestries and mounted weapons.

'They're shameless round here about exploiting King Arthur,' Tarquin said, waving at a painting of the legendary king on the wall beside a standing lamp. 'I mean, there's no proof he even existed, and if he did, he probably didn't live in Tintagel. The castle wasn't even built until five hundred years after the only historical mention of any king with an even comparable name. Doesn't stop them naming it King

Arthur's castle, does it? As shameless as a pigeon dressed as a hawk.' Tarquin pouted. 'Historical blasphemy.'

Lucy laughed. A customer on the next table glanced over, but Tarquin stuck out a tongue at the man and he looked away.

'So,' Tarquin said, 'let's get the awkwardness out of the way. I can tell simply from your body language and the freedom of your laughter that you're enjoying my company, but you'd enjoy it a lot more if my name was Dan, wouldn't you?' Before Lucy could answer, he added, 'And much as I'm delighted to be here with you, I'd rather be talking to a spectacular young man from the Bodmin craft market whose name is Nathaniel and who paints the most exquisite watercolours of coastal panoramas. But alas, he's betrothed to a carpenter named Neil.'

Lucy started laughing again. The man on the next table looked over again, and this time began to laugh, too. He lifted a glass and drunkenly muttered, 'Merry Christmas!'

'I'm sorry to disappoint you,' Lucy said, when she had got herself under control. 'I feel like an idiot, but I can't stop thinking about your brother. I don't even know him that well, and I'm not sure if I'd like him if I did, but whenever I see him I get hot under the collar and I lose the ability to speak.' Suddenly feeling a moment of self-consciousness, and wondering how often Mark had topped up her mulled wine, she added, 'Good God, did I just say that? I sound like a TV drama.'

Tarquin leaned forward, made a flower-shape with his hands, and rested his chin on them as he watched her.

'What a travesty young love is. Do you know what Nathaniel said to me the last time I saw him?'

'Um, no…?'

'"Nine pounds and seventy pence, please",' Tarquin said. 'I bought half a yard of Madras silk to patch Rod and Joe's overalls. The poor boy is entirely unaware of my infatuation.'

Lucy started laughing again. This time she anticipated the man at the next table turning around by leaning over and getting her glass ready for a salute.

'It must be a nightmare,' she said. Then, realising what he had said, she added, 'You patch your staff's overalls with silk?'

Tarquin nodded. 'A man with pride in his clothing will have pride in his work,' he said, then gave a shrug which was almost like a slipping out of character. 'They're used to it. Known them for years. Indeed, Joe's a closet bi but he hasn't come out yet, not even to himself. Trust me, he will in time.'

'I trust you.'

A waitress brought their food. Tarquin, who had announced their entrance with 'The best table please, two specials, and don't forget the locals' discount,' smacked his lips with his fingers as two steaming plates of plaice and chips were set down in front of them. Lucy stared in horror at the monstrous plate, certain she couldn't even eat half of it.

'Tuck in,' Tarquin said, spearing a chip with his fork then taking a tentative bite. 'Delightful,' he said. 'No better place for a first just-friends date, is there?'

'Nowhere in the world,' Lucy agreed.

'Now, let's get down to business. First, my brother.'

Lucy, who had already said more than she felt comfortable with, found herself blushing. 'What about him?'

'I know you said that you liked him, but it sounded like you have some worries about his personality. I'd just like to put them to rest. If there's a finer human being in North Cornwall, I'm yet to meet him. Oh, and that's a far larger sample size than you might think, in case you thought North Cornwall was nothing much other than a few cows and sheep and desolate beaches.' He put down his fork and lifted a hand. 'Okay, North Cornwall in summer. In winter we're not talking all that many people.'

Lucy laughed, then immediately turned to clink glasses with the neighbouring customer, who was also tucking into a huge plate of plaice and chips.

'Do you know where he is tonight?' Tarquin asked.

Lucy shook her head. 'I looked around for him, but I didn't see him.'

'You won't. He's out on the cliffs.'

Lucy frowned. 'What's he doing out there?'

'Keeping watch. Far too many drinkers out tonight. Most people will be sensible, but you're always going to get a few who have a little too much.

And while locals grow up to respect this place, tourists might not. You don't want to be wandering around on those cliffs at night after a skinful, believe me. Dan's out there patrolling up and down, to make sure everyone gets home safely.'

'What is he, some kind of saint?'

Tarquin shook his head. 'Volunteer coastguard.'

'Oh.'

'Denzil asked for volunteers, and Dan was the first to put his hand up,' Tarquin said. 'He loves this area, but he knows how dangerous it can be if you're not sure where you're going. He's out there making sure no one has an accident.'

'That's … really nice of him.'

'He's not that much for talking, is Dan,' Tarquin said. 'He prefers to keep his head down and get on with things.'

Lucy nodded, eating in silence while Tarquin suddenly pulled a phone out of his pocket and began frantically typing a message while a couple of dozen affixed keyrings jingled.

'Sorry,' Tarquin said, suddenly lifting his phone and pointing the camera at Lucy. She blinked as he took a quick snap, then dropped it to the table and resumed typing while Lucy sat there bemused, wondering if she should be offended or not.

'What are you doing?' she asked, taking a sip of the wine Tarquin had ordered.

'Social justice,' Tarquin said.

'What?'

He looked up. 'I'm repairing your honour.'

'Um ... how?'

He turned the phone around to show Lucy's picture. 'You look delightful,' he said. 'Despite what a certain troll might think. I hope you don't mind, but I just shared your picture on Instagram, then linked it to what that Lady Macbeth has been posting about you.'

Lucy was sure she should feel offended or violated, but Tarquin was so earnest she could only feel a strange sense of wonderment, as though she'd fallen down her own rabbit hole and got trapped inside a dream.

'What exactly do you mean?'

'Well, she's been posting about you being the Beast of Bodmin, and admittedly the pictures she's taken of you are less than flattering. I decided to share with my followers that you're not the monster she's making out, and that in fact you are quite delightful.'

'Should I be happy about this?'

Tarquin arched an eyebrow. 'Delighted, my dear.'

'Um, how many followers do you have? Elizabeth Trevellian has a couple of million.'

Tarquin flapped a hand. 'Oh, nothing like that. I'm just past eighty-four k.'

'Eighty-four ... you mean, thousand?'

'Yes, give or take. The quilting community is rampant on social media, wouldn't you know? The average age of my followers must be fifty-plus, and they don't take kindly to rudeness.' He grinned. 'Merry Christmas, Lucy. I've just set an army of quilters onto Elizabeth Trevellian. That poor girl isn't going to know what hit her until she's floundering underneath a veritable mountain of stuffing and silk. Oh, did I just say "floundering"?' Tarquin tapped his plate and started to laugh.

The man on the neighbouring table joined in, then leaned over and drunkenly muttered, 'I ain't cod much to say about that. In fact, I've haddock enough.'

Tarquin gave a dramatic sigh. 'You've really knocked me off my … perch.'

Lucy tried to think of a response using the word "octopus", but couldn't think of anything and instead burst into laughter. After she had finally regained control of herself, she said to Tarquin, 'Thank you for looking out for me. That woman has been the bane of my life these last few days.'

'And she used to be the bane of mine. She played Dan for a fool, and I've never forgiven her. Now that she's back, I don't know what to do. I can't bear the thought of her getting her talons back into him.'

'Perhaps she'll leave once Christmas is over,' Lucy said.

'Maybe. But I hope it's not after breaking Dan's heart all over again. No, I don't want her near him.' Tarquin leaned forward. 'And you know what would help?'

'Um … what?'

'Look, I know Dan likes you. I've seen the way he looks at you, and he has that same goofy awkwardness that you have when you're around each other.'

'No, he doesn't!'

'Oh, he totally does.'

'Totally does,' agreed the man on the next table, who had turned his chair around to join the conversation.

'How could he like me?' Lucy said. 'I laugh like a horse with a cheese-grater stuck in its throat.'

'Only when you're nervous. When you're relaxed, you have a lovely laugh.'

'It's not lovely! It's never been lovely.'

Before Tarquin could respond, the man on the next table lifted a hand. 'Lass,' he said, 'don't be talking like that. When I first heard you laugh, it was like a foghorn coming out of the dark. But, you know what I hear in that laugh?'

'What?'

'Happiness. And you know what makes a person happiest of all?'

Lucy, wondering if she was in some bizarre secretly filmed reality show, downed the last of her wine and said, 'Um, fudge?'

'Yeah, but that's not all. Who doesn't like a bit of fudge, eh? No, it's happiness. Happy makes people happy. When I hear that blessed laugh, it makes me feel all tingly. You've got a gift, lass. Don't keep your mouth shut. Let it come bursting out.'

'Um, I'll try.'

The man on the next table stood up. 'Well, best be getting back to me farm. Cows won't muck out themselves, will they? You have a good night, youngsters, and a Merry Christmas to you both.'

As the man stumbled out, Lucy shook her head. 'Please don't try to match-make me with Dan.'

Tarquin rolled his eyes. 'I'm not planning to. I'm only hoping that you'll get enough of his attention to force Elizabeth Trevellian's fangs off.'

Lucy wasn't sure of anything except that she was drunk. Tarquin was looking at his watch.

'Oh, golly gosh, is that the time? We'd better get going. Karaoke starts at the pub in half an hour. We need to get ringside seats before it gets too packed.'

They headed outside. Lucy pulled out her purse, but Tarquin refused to let her pay anything. She waited for him as he pulled on his jacket, then took his arm and they stepped outside together.

They had gone no more than a couple of steps before something unusual made them both stop in their tracks. Together, they looked up at the little spots flickering through the glow of the restaurant's outside light.

'Huh,' Lucy said, unable to keep a smile off her face. 'It's snowing.'

30

KARAOKE

Lucy, wanting to freshen up before she went to the pub for karaoke, parted ways with Tarquin at the turning to The Lighthouse Keeper and headed back to the holiday park. Her parents, clearly exhausted after the day's endeavours, were slumped on the sofa in front of a Christmas movie playing on low volume. Both were snoring loudly, the dregs of two glasses of port and a half eaten kebab on the coffee table in front of them. Lucy smiled as she tugged down her dad's shirt where it had risen up over his belly, then fetched a blanket from a cupboard and laid it across them.

'Night night,' she whispered, letting her gaze linger on them for a few seconds.

It was just after nine o'clock, so Lucy took a shower, changed her clothes, and drank a quick coffee —the taste boosted by some shamelessly indulgent marshmallows—just to wake herself up a little bit.

Then, unable to resist, she fetched her phone and had a quick look at the social media war currently going on between Elizabeth Trevellian's fanatical horde of followers and Tarquin's smaller but vocal quilter army.

All of it centred on the way she, Lucy, had been portrayed, once as a simple buffoon, and once as a seemingly normal girl enjoying her dinner.

Some of the comments were ridiculous. People had dissected every corner of each picture, debating the most random of things, such as that the restaurant lighting was intentionally dimmed to make her look younger, or that the angle of her nose meant it had been touched up in a photo editor. People had dissected the clothing she wore; items she hadn't even thought about had been dismissed as brands bought only by cheap people, or that the way she had rolled up her sleeves in one picture showed a lack of understanding of the basics of fabric maintenance.

When Lucy got to one ridiculous comment criticizing the length of her fingers, she realised it was time to stop. She looked up to find she had wasted twenty minutes reading pointless criticisms by complete strangers and gave a tired sigh. She couldn't deny that seeing herself ridiculed online was upsetting, but when she looked down at the little plastic box resting on her hand, it all seemed so pointless.

Who cared what someone she had never met and likely would never meet thought about the length of her fingers, or the way she wore her hair, or the depth to which she rolled her sweater's neck? Did it really matter that someone didn't like the blemish on her cheek or thought her lips were too thin?

It was all just a stupid game, and she was wasting precious time getting worked up over something that, in the great scheme of things, didn't matter one jolt.

She glanced up at her parents. What really mattered was what they thought about her, and what she thought about herself.

It was December twenty-third, and it was karaoke night in the pub. Lucy pulled on her jacket and headed out.

It was still snowing outside, although only a little. Lucy walked through a dusting of snow up the farm lane to the high street, where most of the stalls had closed up for the night. Only a couple selling after-hours takeaway food were still operating, but a large number of people still walked up and down the street, some taking pictures, others holding hands.

The Lighthouse Keeper was literally overflowing. As the hideous wail of someone slaughtering *White Christmas* came through open windows, Lucy made her way up through a beer garden filled with people standing around outdoor paraffin heaters, drinking and laughing, and went in through the doors.

Dom from the Bodmin Balloon Club was standing on a chair, spraying a laughing crowd with fake snow from a can as he bellowed and wheezed his way through to the end of the song. To raucous cries he climbed down and passed the microphone over to Jed Penrose, who wore a calamitous homemade snowman costume made from dozens of sheets of A4 paper all stapled together.

'Right, you lot, I hope you enjoyed that. Next up, we have a local legend.' Cheers came from the crowd, but Jed flapped a hand as though patting out flames. 'While it might look like she's risen from the dead, she's still alive and kicking and scaring us all to death. It's the incredible Theresa Burton, who's going to sing, for a change, *Santa, Won't You Rest Your Weary Head*.'

Theresa? Lucy stared. Surely not the terrifying old biddy who ran the holiday park?

To cheers and mock jeers, the elderly holiday park owner stood up from a chair in the corner and made her way through the crowd to the microphone. In a grey sweater and a beige, ankle-length skirt, she was practically the only person in the room not wearing some kind of Christmas-themed attire, but as she took the microphone, she turned to the crowd and bellowed, 'I require complete silence, right now. Those of you who remember me from your school days, don't you forget what happens when you talk in my classes!'

Half of the crowd immediately hushed. The other half, probably holidaymakers, slowly fell quiet. 'What happens?' someone nearby asked, turning to Col, the bearded chap Lucy remembered sleeping in the pub on her first night here. He looked a lot more awake this time than he had before, his eyes wide as he stared at the old woman climbing precariously up on to a chair.

'She stares at you until you cry,' he muttered. 'She doesn't blink, mate. Ever.'

'Like, *ever*?'

'Thirty-seven minutes, mate. That's the longest someone ever held out. And it broke him. You see him wandering about the village sometimes, picking up bits of litter and laughing like a maniac.'

'Really?'

'Just don't meet her eyes and you'll be okay.'

Theresa cleared her throat as the music began. It was an old song, one Lucy recognised but hadn't heard in years. She shook her head, trying to recall the singer's name, as Theresa began to sing, a clear, ringing, note-perfect version of the old Christmas classic. The crowd was silent as everyone watched, transfixed. Several people nearby covered their mouths, others wiped tears from their eyes. Theresa, one arm lifted skyward, brought the song to a rousing conclusion, holding one long note that she cut off with a sudden flourish.

'Thank you very much,' she said, her lips curling into a hint of a smile as the crowd burst into a spontaneous round of enthusiastic applause. Several people were openly crying, and one drunken old man pushed through the crowd and held out a beer mat for her autograph. He looked genuinely disappointed when she waved him away.

'A Merry Christmas to you all,' she said, climbing

down from the chair. 'I'll be getting home now and leaving this silly party to you youngsters. Just remember your resolutions this year: be polite, be nice, study hard … and stay off my land.'

The crowd clapped as Theresa made her way through to the door and vanished into the night. Jed Penrose was smiling and shaking his head as he watched her leave. Suddenly remembering what he was doing, he glanced down at the sheet of paper in his hand and called out the next name.

'She's quite something, isn't she?' came a voice Lucy recognised, and she turned to find Denzil Porthleven standing beside her, a pint of bitter in his hands. 'And quite a character, too.'

'I would never have guessed she could sing like that.'

'She was a professional singer, way back in the fifties and sixties,' Denzil said. 'She had a Christmas hit in the States in the early sixties and some say she's lived off the royalties since then, that holiday park being little more than a tax write-off. Of course, most people round here remember her as the dragon who taught Class Six in Tintagel Primary School. We weren't allowed to call her Miss Burton. It was "Miss Theresa, Miss." And heaven help you if you pronounced her name with a hard T. You got kept back after school, where you were subjected to The Stare.' Denzil actually shuddered. 'She shows up once a year at karaoke to sing her hit and remind us all that the bogeyman still exists.'

'Her voice was amazing.'

'Even to this day, she gets more letters than anyone else in the village, all fan mail from right across the world. Forget about Elizabeth Trevellian. The most famous export out of Tintagel—after fudge—is Theresa Burton.'

Lucy smiled. 'Must be a bone of contention.'

Denzil laughed. 'Oh, believe me, Elizabeth Trevellian has no idea. That girl has little idea about anything outside her own range of vision.'

'Lucy, there you are!' came a familiar voice from across the pub. She turned to find Tarquin waving at her from the bar. Rod and Joe were with him, as were a couple of other people she had seen working up by the cricket field.

She made her way over, and Tarquin greeted her warmly before introducing her to his friends. Jed Penrose called over to take their drinks order, then Tarquin held up a clipboard. 'What are you going to sing?' he asked. 'No excuses. Pick something.'

'Oh, I'm not sure—'

Tarquin smiled. 'Either you pick something, or I pick something for you. Look, if you're nervous, I'd be happy to duet.'

Be positive, Lucy reminded herself. 'Okay, give me that. This is the list of songs already done, right?'

'That's right.'

'And these are the ones I can choose from?'

'You've got it.'

Lucy's eyes scanned the list. It was in order of popularity, with all the biggest Christmas songs near the top of the list. As well as a separate list of all the people who had signed up to sing, Jed had ticked off the songs sung or queued to make things easier. Lucy turned over the page, skimming down the list, quickly reaching the bottom half where she recognised almost nothing.

A sudden thought came to her. It was probably the drink talking, but it was Christmas, so she didn't really care. She ran a finger down to the very bottom of the list, to a song which had never been sung before. She didn't even remember hearing it, but the artist was familiar, so she nodded and held up the clipboard to Tarquin.

'That one,' she said. 'I'll do that one.'

Tarquin frowned. 'Are you sure? I mean, it's probably not popular for a reason. Look, no one's done Wizzard or Donny Osmond yet—'

'That one,' Lucy said, defiant. 'But get me another drink first.'

Tarquin laughed. 'High fives all round for bravery,' he suddenly yelled, lifting his hands in the air for each of his friends to slap. Lucy grinned and took her own turn, then passed the clipboard back.

The next person up was Joe, who did a solid rendition of *Santa Claus is Coming to Town*, complete with bizarre train motions which got the whole crowd on their feet and mimicking him. Next were a couple of older people doing slower fifties songs for which Jed lowered the lights in order for couples to slow dance. Lucy, getting increasingly weary after a day that felt endless, rested her chin on her hands and wondered absently what Dan was doing. Was he still out on the cliffs, like a human lighthouse, guiding people safely home? She wondered if he wanted some company, whether he would mind if she wrapped herself up in her coat and went out there in the Tintagel wilds to stand with him, to—

'Frances Lucy Scullion-Drake!' bellowed Jed, frowning at the name. 'Um, you're up.'

'Go on, Lucy,' Tarquin hissed, patting her on the back and then letting out an earsplitting wolf whistle as she climbed down off her stool and made her way through the crowd.

Jed helped her climb up on to the chair to a series of cheers and catcalls. 'You only needed to write your first name,' he whispered, holding her hand until she had found her balance. Then, lifting the microphone, he said, 'Now, to sing the *Postman Pat Christmas Special Theme Closing Credits*, we have …. Frances—um, I mean Lucy!'

The crowd clapped as the familiar tune from Lucy's childhood began to rattle out of the speakers. By the bar, Tarquin and his friends were jovially clapping along. Lucy didn't ever remember watching the cartoon's Christmas special, so she glanced at the karaoke monitor set up on a table in front of her, waiting for the lyrics to start.

Nothing happened. After a few seconds, a line flashed up simply saying, Instrumental: 245 Seconds.

'You did know it was an instrumental, didn't you, lass?' Jed hissed, looking up from where he sat by her feet. 'That's why no one sings it, eh. Perhaps you could just do some gestures or something.'

Lucy felt her cheeks turning cherry red. The crowd was clapping and cheering as though realising her karaoke newbie's error, and there was nothing she could do but ride it out. The tune was familiar, and the booze had its grip on her, so Lucy took a deep breath, closed her eyes, and then began to sing her own made up version over the top, complete with Christmas lyrical additions.

'Whisky's in the stocking, and Postman Pat has presents in his van!'

The crowd bellowed with laughter. Lucy, running out of things to say, began to make cat noises and paw at the air. The crowd roared. Lucy scanned the faces, wondering how many were sober enough to remember this abomination in the morning—

Her smile dropped.

In the shadows by the door, Elizabeth Trevellian stood, holding up a smartphone, laughing as she pointed it at Lucy.

You won't get yet another one over on me, she thought, gripping the microphone tightly and taking a deep breath. It was nearly closing time. There might only be a couple of songs left.

'Merrry Chriiiiiistmas!' she bellowed, her voice cracking in the middle, causing a sudden rift in the laughter as people reached to cover their ears. Moments later they were laughing again, but when Lucy looked around, Elizabeth Trevellian had gone.

'Thank you,' Jed said, as the music ended and Lucy climbed down from the stool. 'That'll certainly be one that everyone will remember in years to come.'

He patted her on the back and then turned to his list to call the next singer as Lucy made her way back to where Tarquin stood.

'Absolutely classic!' he said, laughing. 'I've never seen anything quite like that before.'

Lucy frowned. 'How many quilter friends do you have left?' she asked. 'Elizabeth was here, over by the door. She was filming me.' With a sigh she added, 'I think Team Lucy just fell behind again.'

31

SURFING

'Honestly,' Valerie said, passing Lucy a piece of toast, 'I think life would be so much better if we didn't have people filming everything. 'Do you know that studies have found a link between depression and the extent to which people photograph everything? Memories no longer become rose-tinted like they used to. Everything is remembered in so much stark detail that insecurities which would otherwise have been left behind, not constantly remembered, are reflected in the photographs from which people can no longer escape.'

Lucy yawned, then took a sip of her hot chocolate. 'Is that so?'

'I mean, what happens in the pub should stay in the pub, if I had to put it in layman's terms.'

'So you've seen the video?'

Valerie smiled. 'Dear, I thought it was hilarious. I mean, who would think to do an instrumental children's TV theme tune at a karaoke night and then make up silly things to go over the top?'

'I think it's called free-styling,' Alan said, pulling back the curtain to the bathroom area to reveal himself with a towel wrapped around his ample waist and a dressing gown hung over his shoulders. He lifted a hand to his ear and made DJ scratching gestures with his other hand, until suddenly forced to lunge for the towel as it threatened to break away.

'Dad, firstly, when did you get so "street"?' Lucy said, smiling. 'And secondly, couldn't you get dressed first?'

'Sorry, love, I'm in a bit of a rush this morning. Got work to do up at the cricket ground.'

'What work?' Valerie said.

'Top secret stuff.' Alan tapped the side of his nose. 'So, you had a good night, then?'

'Peaks and troughs,' Lucy said. She rubbed her head, wondering if she would feel worse about Elizabeth's video when her hangover cleared. At the moment she felt only a gentle sense of amusement, even though Melanie had messaged her this morning to say Lucy had shown up as a video meme on one of her social media pages. Without any effort on her part, it seemed Lucy had become an internet star overnight. Despite Tarquin's quilter army coming to her aid, Elizabeth's video, which had simply held the caption *"I have no words"*, had been shared thousands of times.

'What are your plans for the day, dear?' Valerie asked. 'This morning I was asked to help deliver

Christmas puddings to the local nursing homes, but I thought we could meet for lunch. It's Christmas Eve, after all.'

Lucy smiled. 'I'm going to the Christmas surf down on the beach,' she said. 'I thought I might paddle off into the sunset.'

'It's a bit early in the day for that, dear,' Valerie said.

'You're going surfing?' Alan asked. 'In December?'

Lucy shrugged. 'I think it's ceremonial. A quick in and out. I imagine the water's pretty cold.'

Valerie shook her head. 'The water … have you been outside this morning?'

Lucy shook her head.

'Well, perhaps you should go and take a look.'

Lucy could barely remember getting home last night. After a few more songs, plus an impromptu bout of carol singing in the pub car park, she had headed back to the holiday park, but as soon as she was alone her thoughts had closed in, and she remembered little of the journey before collapsing into bed. Now, though, as she went to the front of the tent and unzipped the doors, she couldn't help but gasp in surprise.

'It's been snowing all night,' Valerie said. 'Ellie was right after all. The forecast is still saying it's clear, but I think we can both see it's quite wrong.'

'Wow.' Lucy reached for her boots. 'I'm going to take a walk.'

'Be careful you don't slip.'

Lucy could barely hear anything her mother was saying. She was transfixed by the wintery scene in front of her, the snow-topped houses, hedgerows, and trees, the perfect blanket of white which covered the ground, and the steady patter of the snow as it continued to fall all around her.

'Look, Val,' Alan said from behind her as she stepped outside and pulled up the zipper. 'The forecast is still saying it's clear….'

Lucy found Theresa outside the farmhouse, scraping paths in the ankle-deep snow with a plastic spade.

'Merry Christmas,' Lucy greeted her. 'Do you need any help?'

'Do I look like a charity?' Theresa scowled. 'You call this snow? You kids don't know anything at all. In my day we had to walk fifteen miles for a glass of fresh water.'

Lucy gave her a sweet smile. 'Would you like anything from the shops?'

'Think I can't walk there on my own two legs?'

'Well, have a nice day.'

Lucy walked away, humming *Santa, Won't You Rest Your Weary Head* as she headed for the farm lane leading up to the main entrance. Just as she passed the end of a parked tractor, she turned and looked back over her shoulder. Theresa, who had been standing and watching her, dropped a secret smile and turned grumpily back to her snow-clearing. Lucy gave her a little wave and then carried on her way.

It was barely eight o'clock, but the high street was

a hive of activity. Everywhere, people were clearing the pavements of snow and shoveling it into neat piles alongside the road. Lucy heard the jingle of a bell and looked up just as the reindeer-pulled sled made its way down the street, sliding smoothly on steel runners. People stopped what they were doing as the reindeer came past, some crying out with delight or waving at the group of children sitting behind the driver.

Up at the cricket ground, Lucy found a number of bleary-eyed workers in the pavilion getting ready to open everything up. Dom from the Bodmin Balloon Club was tucking into a plate of mince pies, while Rebecca was attempting to repair one of her ginger bobs which had come undone at some point. Lucy offered to help, sitting Rebecca at a table in front of her and then following the girl's instructions to get the hair back into place.

'Don't know what you're worried about,' Dom said. 'Just get a Christmas hat over it.'

'I don't want it being lopsided,' Rebecca answered with a grin.

Denzil Porthleven was outside, holding a clipboard and talking to a group of stage hands. Lucy filled a paper cup with coffee from a filter and took it out to him.

'How's everything going?' she asked.

Denzil laughed. 'Just wondering if we have anything on today's lineup which can compete with your performance last night,' he said. 'I've had six people already asking if the Christmas Cat Lady will be performing.'

Lucy winced. 'I think she's retired,' she said. 'But I suppose you never know when she might make a cameo. Christmas spirit and all that.'

'I look forward to it. Is your dad up?'

'He was just getting there when I left. I think he's coming up here soon.'

'Good. I need to talk to him.'

'What about?'

Denzil smiled. 'I'm afraid it's a secret.'

'What are you two planning?'

'I really can't say. It was your dad's idea, though. Honestly, he's really taken the bull by the horns. I didn't expect any of the sponsors to be so hands on, let alone have so many good ideas.'

'I'm intrigued.'

'Trust me, it'll be spectacular.'

'I can't wait.'

Denzil excused himself to go and organise the day's schedule in the big top, so for a while Lucy helped a group of people clearing the snow from the car park to allow the buses to get in and out. It was still falling, now about ten centimetres deep, and the group sang Christmas songs as they worked.

'Looks like the snowman competition will go ahead after all,' said Joe. 'It was a provisional on the schedule, but I'd say we have enough. Much more and we'll be snowed in.'

'Are you going down to the Christmas surf?' Lucy said, glancing over her shoulder to check a clock on the wall of the pavilion. 'It starts at ten.'

'Haven't missed it since I was old enough to

swim,' Joe said. 'Must be going on twenty-five years. Although it's usually on Christmas Day. I'll probably go down there again tomorrow, but this morning is for the holidaymakers. Not sure if that's a good idea or not.'

'Why not?'

'Well, it's cold. And you know, it's only a bit of fun. You don't want anyone taking it too seriously, going out too far, trying to catch something out back, that sort of thing. It's pretty cold, and winter swells are unpredictable.'

'I'll be careful.'

Joe laughed. 'You only need to get your feet wet then run back up the beach and grab a mince pie.'

'Sounds great.'

They carried on digging for another half an hour before Joe excused himself to go and check on the various amusement rides before they opened. Despite the falling snow, the car park was now accessible, and Lucy helped Jed Penrose mark the way in by planting red poles with reindeer-design ticker tape tied to the top into the piles of snow now lining the entrance. Just for good measure, they then built a snowman with a grinning gravel mouth and a stick for an arm which waved up and down in the breeze as though to welcome visitors.

They had only just finished when Frederika's bus pulled in laden with tourists from a local campsite. As they bustled off, most of them decked out in Christmas hats, Frederika leaned out of the side window. 'I hope you're ready,' she shouted to Lucy. 'Today's the big day!'

After the karaoke debacle last night, Lucy had nearly forgotten that she had promised to join Frederika's yodeling troupe on the main stage tonight. She felt a tingle of nerves, but figured she couldn't possibly embarrass herself any more than she had already.

'I'm looking forward to it!' she shouted back.

It was nearly time to head to the beach. Lucy looked around for Joe, wondering if he was planning to walk down, but there was no sign of him. Instead, she headed back along the high street by herself, pausing outside the fudge stall to say good morning and Merry Christmas to Klaus, who was building daunting piles of fudge inside the display cabinet.

'Where are you going this fine Christmas morning?' he asked her.

'To the beach. The Christmas surf. Are you coming?'

Klaus laughed. 'Cold water at Christmas? I'll stay with the warm fudge. Mark's going down, though. If you hang on, I'll see if he's ready. Can you hold the stall for a minute?'

Klaus disappeared inside, and Lucy dutifully stood beside the stall, waiting for customers. She had hardly been there a minute when a family with two little children approached. The girl, no more than eleven years old, took one look at her and ducked behind her mother.

'That's her,' she whispered, loud enough for Lucy to hear. 'That's the dancing cat lady.'

Elizabeth Trevellian's fans had to be younger than Lucy realised. The girl was barely in secondary school yet had found a role model in the snobby, unpleasant woman who had been making Lucy's life hell these last few days. She thought about denying it, but then a sudden idea came to mind.

She squatted down. 'Nice spot,' she said to the girl. 'Would you like a picture?'

The girl's face suddenly brightened. 'Really?'

Lucy lifted a paw and made a mewing sound which caused her cheeks to redden. 'Sure.'

The girl came over while the father pulled out a camera and aimed his shot. Lucy lifted her hands into claws and grimaced like a snarling cat. The girl gave a thumbs-up and smiled.

'Thanks so much,' the girl said.

'No problem.'

'Can I put it on the internet so my friends can see it? Is that okay?'

Lucy deliberated only a moment. 'Sure,' she said. 'Just mention where you saw me. Right, would you like some fudge? I'll give you a ten percent discount if you buy over a kilo.'

'That would be fantastic,' the father said, ignoring a scowl from the mother aimed at his stomach. 'Fifteen percent if we buy two?'

Lucy shrugged. 'Why not? It's Christmas.'

She was just finishing up the sale as Klaus and Mark came out of the shop door. Klaus lifted an

218

eyebrow as he saw the family heading back down to the high street, the dad carrying a large paper bag with Bale's Fudge & Confectionery on the side.

'You're getting us underway already?' Mark asked.

Lucy grinned. 'The dad even bought a t-shirt,' she said.

'Nice work. I do believe you've earned a break. Are you ready to head down to the beach?'

Lucy nodded. She noticed Mark was wearing a wetsuit under his clothes. 'How long are you planning to stay in?' she asked.

'Dan and me are on lifeguard duty,' Mark said. 'To make sure no one goes too far out.'

They walked together down to the end of the high street, where they found another of the Swiss minibuses waiting outside the Castle Hotel to ferry people a couple of miles to a local surfing beach. In the snow, the journey along the twisting coastal road was as thrilling as any amusement park ride Lucy had been on, but the driver seemed completely unconcerned as they occasionally slipped or lurched, each time drawing gasps from the passengers.

On the foreshore, a group of people had already built a large fire, and nearby were several tables containing wetsuits in various sizes. Lined up on the beach in front were a couple of dozen surfboards. Some were barely a metre long, clearly designed for children, while others were almost boats, twice the length of a man.

Col from the pub, wearing a tatty Quiksilver sweater, was helping people select wetsuits, while Rod was handing out surfboards and giving a few hints before the tourists got ready to take them down to the beach. The sea itself was choppy, a mess of whitewater with a decent breeze blowing from offshore. With the snow being turned into churning eddies which made visibility poor, Lucy felt that even five minutes would be too long, but from the smiles all around her, as well as the presence of a number of grizzled, aging surfers already suited and ready to go with their battered surfboards tucked under their arms, she could tell it was a long-held tradition.

Mark came over and helped Lucy pick out a suit that was the right size before leading her to a line of changing cubicles on the foreshore. The suit's rubber was stretchy but hard and it pressed tight against her skin. By the time she emerged, her arms were aching from the effort of pulling it on, and she now understood why surfers were always so muscular. Just getting the suit on was a workout in itself before you ever got near the water.

The rest of the group had assembled near the shoreline. Lucy estimated about thirty people in all, some wearing sodden Christmas hats or strings of tinsel tied around their shoulders. Lucy looked around for Dan, but he wasn't standing among the group. Then she remembered what Mark had said, and looked out to sea. Beyond the first line of waves, a man sat on a surfboard, watching the beach.

He would have been difficult to see except that he wore a fluorescent yellow jacket over his wetsuit. Even then, with the rise and fall of the waves and the flurrying snow he was continually vanishing from sight like a light blinking on and off. As she watched, though, Dan lifted a hand and waved.

Smiling, Lucy instinctively waved back. He seemed to be looking directly at her, but just as she dropped her hand, she smelled something unusual at her left shoulder.

Perfume.

'You're optimistic, aren't you?' Elizabeth Trevellian said, sneering at her. The model wore a brand new wetsuit and had a brand new surfboard under her arm, both prominently displaying corporate sponsor logos. Her hair had been plaited into two long strands, and even on this wild and windswept beach in the middle of a snowstorm, she looked absolutely gorgeous.

'I was stretching my arm,' Lucy said, her cheeks burning despite the cold.

'If you say so,' Elizabeth said, then lifted her own arm and waved out at Dan. 'Coo-ee, Dan, I'm coming!' she called, in a voice so saccharine sweet Lucy could have spooned it into her father's hot chocolate.

'Ready, go!' shouted Mark from across the beach. Laughing and cheering, the surfers rushed for the waves. Snow continued to swirl all around them. Elizabeth broke into a run down a triangle of sand between the rocky foreshore and the tumbling shore breakers, quickly leaving Lucy in her wake. Lucy rushed to catch up, but by the time she reached the water, Elizabeth was on her board, paddling hard out into the surf.

Lucy wasn't prepared for the shock as her feet touched the water. A rush of cold danced up her legs, and despite the wetsuit she felt the cold permeate through her. She took a few steps farther in until she was up to her knees, then lowered the board into the water, angling it away from the first tumbling line of white water heading her way.

The wave was tiny, but it hit her with surprising force, water sloshing up over her waist. She let out a shrill cry which turned into a whooping laugh as a second line of swell cascaded over her chest.

'Got to get your shoulders wet!' shouted Joe, standing nearby, as he helped a young boy get on to his board before pushing him onto the next wave.

Some people were already getting out, catching tiny waves strong enough only to move them a few feet as they leaned on their boards with their hands. A few others, mostly locals, had waded out farther, some deep enough that they were now sitting on their boards, trying to catch waves yet to break. Lucy looked out toward the horizon, but from here she couldn't see Dan behind the line of oncoming swell. As she bobbed over a wave though, she caught sight of Elizabeth Trevellian, paddling hard over a rising swell far beyond the rest of the group.

The girl clearly knew what she was doing. Lucy, wincing at each slosh of water and not feeling any warmer, even though she knew her body ought to have got used to the cold by now, felt woefully useless.

In defiance she waded out a little farther, but the next wave hit her right on the break. As freezing water sloshed over her face and poured down her neck through a gap in the zip she now realised she hadn't done up tightly enough, Lucy decided she was ready to get out. She glanced across at the rest of the revellers still in the surf, copying them as they leaned on their boards just as the wave arrived, then jumped on and began paddling.

The wave hit her from behind and the board rushed forward. Lucy paddled frantically, but the board was off-straight. The wave took it sideways, rolling her off. She sat up gasping as water sloshed over her face. She found Mark standing over her, the water barely up to his knees. He reached down and helped her up, a wide grin on his face.

'Merry Christmas,' he said. 'You're officially Cornish now.'

'Thanks.'

Lucy climbed out of the water and retrieved her board from the shallows nearby. Feeling like she had just run an Arctic marathon, she staggered back up the foreshore to where the others waited. Joe laughed as he handed her a towel.

'Nice duck dive,' he said. 'You're a natural.'

'It's so cold!'

'Ah, but you can't beat a Christmas surf. Makes you feel alive, doesn't it?'

Lucy nodded. 'I suppose you could say that.'

She sat down on a rock beside Joe with the towel wrapped around her. Almost everyone was out now.

She watched as a bearded figure she guessed was Col caught a decent-sized wave, jumped to his feet and rode it back to the beach, putting in a couple of neat turns for good measure.

'Now we just have to wait for the poser,' Joe said with a sigh.

At first Lucy thought he meant Dan, still sitting out behind the breakers on his board, but then she noticed another figure moving through the waves.

Elizabeth Trevellian.

'She's pretty good, isn't she?' Lucy said, forcing herself to be nice, but unable to shake a desire to see Elizabeth get dunked.

Joe sighed as he nodded. 'She was Cornish Girls Under-15s Champion,' he said. 'That was how she got noticed in the first place. She knows what she's doing. But that's not all that she's doing, if you know what I mean.'

Lucy said nothing. Her eyes scanned the clifftop, and spotted Shawn sitting in the grass a little way off the meandering coast path, a camera pressed to his eye. Lucy glanced back at Elizabeth just in time to see her catch a decent roller, leap to her feet and execute a neat turn before pulling out of the wave before it broke.

A few locals gave Elizabeth a lazy sarcastic clap. Some were standing up, clearly waiting for her to finish so they could go home. Mark was standing halfway down to the beach, hands on his hips, shaking his head.

'She's waiting for something spectacular,' Joe said,

then nodded. 'Looks like she's going to get it, too. There's a big swell coming in.' Lucy couldn't see it, but Joe pointed at the horizon. 'See how the water's less choppy out there and seems to have those lines of shadow? That's a set. Big one. It'll go right under where Dan's sitting, but Elizabeth's right where it'll break.'

'Will she know?'

'Oh yeah. That girl's used to the water. She's no fool.'

The swell had begun to steepen as it passed under where Dan still sat. Elizabeth spotted it as the nearest wave made a crest, dropping to her board and paddling out over the first wave before it broke. A loud crash sounded as the first wave broke, then, as the spray cleared, Elizabeth became visible once more, paddling hard onto the steepening wall of the second wave in the set. She caught it just as it crested and began to break, curling over behind her as her board raced down its silvery face.

'Eight-footer,' Joe muttered. 'Nice.'

With catlike agility, Elizabeth sprang to her feet, immediately carving the board back up the face of the wave then cutting down into a steep drop. She looked about to disappear in the water, before, at the last moment, hacking the board around and repeating the same loop as before.

Gasps of awe and claps of appreciation came from the group. Lucy caught Joe and Col exchange a look: both rolled their eyes.

Elizabeth's wave was dying, fading into white

water. She dropped down into the water and Lucy waited to see her paddling back out to catch the next swell coming in.

A few seconds passed, but Elizabeth didn't reappear. A few people lifted hands to shade their eyes. Then, as though it had been caught underwater, Elizabeth's board bobbed upward.

Of the girl there was no sign.

In an instant Mark was running for the shoreline, waving his hands over his head and hollering to Dan. Lucy watched Dan drop flat onto his board, powerful arms propelling him forward through the surf as he cut across the water in the direction of Elizabeth's riderless board.

'I think this is serious,' Joe said, jumping up. He waved at Col and the two of them sprinted down to where their boards lay, snatched them up, and ran for the water.

Murmurs of unease moved through the crowd. Lucy climbed onto a rock to try to get a better view. Dan reached Elizabeth's board and jumped down into the water. Mark was halfway out to him, standing up in the surf, his wetsuit still pulled down around his waist, seemingly unaffected by the cold. Joe and Col were paddling steadily out, while a couple of other surf club members had run to a tatty hut and retrieved a foldable stretcher.

'She's drowned,' someone nearby said. 'Oh my, on Christmas as well. How awful.'

Lucy's heart was hammering, taking back everything bad she had ever thought about Elizabeth

Trevellian, despite the way the girl had treated her. She would gladly be called the Beast of Bodmin every day for the rest of her life if Elizabeth could only be all right. She jumped up and down, wishing she didn't feel so useless—

Dan appeared out of the water, something clutched to his chest. A cheer rose from the crowd as he held Elizabeth close. He pulled the girl on to his surfboard and paddled them into a small wave just about to break, steering them as the wave brought the board into the beach.

Mark met him in the shore break, helping him to climb off. Elizabeth lay inert, her face turned to the side. Col and Joe quickly joined them, and together they carried Elizabeth up above the water line.

'Do we need the air ambulance?' Joe said to Mark, as they set the board carrying Elizabeth down. The girl wasn't moving. Dan leaned over her, putting an ear to her mouth, then placing both hands over her chest and pressing down. He repeated the gesture, and then pressed again. The tension all around was unbearable, with complete strangers hugging each other for comfort.

Then, with a sudden gasp, Elizabeth sat up, coughing as she leaned forward into Dan's arms. He held her, patting her back. Her eyes darted around the assembled group, which had begun to clap and cheer.

'Are you all right?' Dan asked, lifting her head to look at her. 'We can call the air ambulance to take you to Derriford—'

Elizabeth gave a frantic shake of her head, then

gave another little cough. 'No, I'm fine, really. I've had worse. I'm so sorry, I thought I could get out, but my leash must have got caught … you saved my life, Dan. I'm indebted to you. Thank you. Thank you so much.'

Then, with the crowd cheering, she leaned forward, and pulled Dan into a powerful kiss.

32

TALENT SHOW

'I'LL HAVE ANOTHER ONE. DOUBLE. WHATEVER IT is, I don't care. Double it.'

Tarquin put a hand on her arm. At least she thought it was Tarquin's, but there were at least three of him now, and she couldn't be sure if he was really there or a figment of her imagination.

'Don't you think you've drunk enough? It's only lunchtime, and if you drink too much more you won't be able to yodel tonight.'

The statement was so absurd Lucy couldn't help but break into a spontaneous fit of wild laughter. She had images of The Lighthouse Keeper emptying, but whether it really did or not she couldn't be sure; she could barely see the hands at the ends of her arms.

'She faked it, Tarquin,' she said. 'I saw him, up on the cliff. Shawn, the photo chap. He was clicking away the whole time. Now she's put it on her social pages and all her fans are swooning over it.'

Saved by an old flame, read the caption. Three pictures, one of Elizabeth being pulled out of the water, one of Dan holding her in his arms, and another of their kiss. Already a couple of thousand people had commented on what a perfect couple they seemed. Probably more, but Lucy had left her phone somewhere and could no longer check.

'She faked it,' she said again. 'She didn't even need help taking off her wetsuit, although she made a meal out of it.'

Tarquin shook his head. 'I don't doubt it. This is Elizabeth Trevellian through and through. Exploiting others for personal gain. I imagine she'll be sponsoring wetsuits before the end of January.'

'Dan's so nice,' Lucy wailed. 'He's wasted on such a conniving … so-and-so as her.'

'Then stop drinking and do something about it,' Tarquin said. 'It's Christmas. Tell Dan that you like him and hopefully we can banish that woman from this place forever.'

'It's too late,' Lucy moaned. 'I'm hammered now. There's no way. It's best for me to just stay here and drown my sorrows.'

'Oh no you're not,' Tarquin said, a little smile appearing on his blurry face.

'Not what?'

'Not drunk.'

'What do you mean?'

'You've only had two drinks. For the rest I had Jed switch out the booze for a bit of Christmas spice.'

'You mean—'

'I mean, pull yourself together and come with me to the cricket ground. "Operation be cooler and more attractive than Elizabeth Trevellian" is officially underway.'

～

Despite Tarquin's revelation, the placebo effect left Lucy slipping and sliding in the ankle-deep snow as they made their way up to the cricket ground. By the time they reached it, though, Lucy's head was finally beginning to clear, and only the morose sense of disappointment at letting the ghastly social media starlet get one over on her yet again hung over her like a low-flying blimp.

'What do we do?' she asked Tarquin as they paused beside a signboard detailing the day's itinerary.

'There,' he said. 'If you can do well in that, word will get out. It's a start.'

'A talent contest?'

Tarquin shrugged. '"All welcome",' he read. '"Just show up and show us what you can do. Prize is a fitted bathroom carpet from Drake's Carpets of Bristol." See? Just show up and go on.'

'I'm pretty sure I'd be breaking the entry rules, being the daughter of the sponsor and all that, but why not?'

'All you need is some sort of talent. What can you do better than anyone else?'

Lucy frowned. 'I'm not sure,' she said.

'Thank you kindly, lad,' Denzil Porthleven said into a microphone. 'One more round of applause for Tommy Craddock and his, um, Social Commentary Bears.'

The crowd of a couple of hundred mostly elderly people clapped politely as a dour-faced schoolboy lifted his puppet show theatre and carried it off into the shadows behind the stage curtain.

'Next up,' Denzil Porthleven said, forcing a smile, 'is the amazing Lucy, and her, um, pen twirling.'

As Lucy reluctantly climbed onto the stage amidst a series of muted claps, she grimaced at Tarquin, who spread his arms wide and mouthed, 'It's Christmas.'

She made her way to the centre of the stage as Denzil turned up the speakers playing Christmas background music. Lucy, glad it was cold enough to stop her blushing, lifted a biro she had found backstage and began to twirl it across her fingers as she had done a thousand times during quiet mornings at work. As talents went, it was pretty unimpressive, but a few kids in the front row were leaning forward and frowning as though entertained.

'It's Christmas,' she repeated to herself, forcing a smile.

Then one little girl began to point as she nudged the girl beside her. 'It's her,' she hissed, loud enough for Lucy to hear. 'It's the dancing cat lady.'

The effect of Elizabeth Trevellian's social reach

rippled out over the crowd. 'Do the dance!' someone shouted. 'Do the dance!'

Sober, Lucy might have fled from the stage, but she still felt a little tingle from her gin and tonics. She tossed the pen to the girl in the front row, who squealed with delight as she caught it. Out of the corner of her eye, Lucy spotted Tarquin fiddling with a smartphone as he squatted by the speakers. A moment later, the background music abruptly cut off and the *Postman Pat Christmas Special Theme* began. Lucy, no longer caring how ridiculous she looked, began to prance back and forth across the stage, doing her cat-zombie impression to the delight of the children in the audience and the bemused horror of the adults. The girl who had received the pen jumped to her feet and began to mimic Lucy's performance, quickly followed by others.

By the time the song was over, Lucy, wondering if she wouldn't have a successful career as a clown, had more than thirty children copying her bizarre, spontaneously invented dance.

The song ended, throwing her immediately back into obscurity. Lucy climbed down off the stage and slumped down into a chair beside a beaming Tarquin.

'Beautiful,' he said, holding up his phone. 'I got a video. Do I have your permission to post it online?'

Lucy put her head in her hands. 'Do as you want,' she said. 'I'm starting to feel like my life no longer belongs to me.'

Tarquin clicked his fingers. 'Ah, that moment of revelation,' he said. 'None of us belong to ourselves, do we? We only exist as people perceive us.' He patted her knee. 'Let's just wait for the voting, shall we? I hope they hurry up, though. The generator on the chocolate crepe stall is on the blink and I need to go give it a quick tweak.'

Voting ballots were passing around the crowd. Lucy sat among the other performers and tried to think positive thoughts as Tarquin grinned into his phone.

'Oh, look,' he said, holding it up. 'You've made the BBC News. A new Christmas dance craze. It doesn't name you, unfortunately. It just mentions Elizabeth and her social media presence.'

'There's a surprise.'

Tarquin frowned. 'Oh, that heathen.'

'What is it?'

'It says here that she's in a relationship with a local surfer. Such callous untruths.'

'Maybe she is,' Lucy sighed. 'I mean, what's not for Dan to like? He had a relationship with her before, and she's even richer and more beautiful than she was then.'

'She's as shallow as a dry river and as hollow as a used toilet roll tube,' Tarquin said. 'That's why Dan won't be interested.'

'He didn't seem to be fighting too hard when she kissed him.'

Tarquin opened his mouth to reply, but Denzil had appeared on stage again with a piece of paper in his hands. He called for quiet, then gave another grim smile.

'Well, thank you very much to all our competitors,' he said. 'It was a wonderful talent contest and I hope all of you take your skills and use them for great things in later life. Now, I shall read the results. With eighty-seven votes, the winner by a considerable margin is Lucy with her random chicken dance.'

'Cat dance!' Tarquin shouted.

'Cat dance,' Denzil said. 'Unfortunately, due to her being the daughter of the event's sponsor, the rules require that she be disqualified. In her place, the new winner is Tommy Craddock and his Social Commentary Bears, with nine votes.'

The boy jumped up out of his seat, two bears on sticks dressed as politicians bouncing up with him. He waved at the crowd as he made his way onto the stage.

'Well done, Tommy,' Denzil said. 'You've won a fitted bathroom carpet for your family, courtesy of Drake's Carpets of Bristol.' A jovial cheer came from the crowd, which did nothing for the dour look on Tommy Craddock's face. Denzil cleared his throat, then added, 'Oh, and a Christmas Cadbury's Selection Box. Well done again.'

With the event over, the crowd began to disperse. Outside, the snow had got heavier, and with the light fading, the rings of Christmas lights had come on, turning the cricket ground into a Christmas winter wonderland. Lucy stood and regarded it all for a couple of minutes, her hands tucked into her pockets, the Christmas hat pulled down to keep the cold off her ears.

It was delightful, and with the Christmas Market on the high street stretching for nearly a mile, she doubted that even the famous Christmas market towns of Germany or perhaps Lapland itself would struggle to hold a candle in comparison. It was just a shame she had no one to share it with—

'Lucy.'

The sound of the familiar voice sent a prickle of nerves down her back. She squeezed her eyes shut as though to give herself strength, then opened them again and turned around.

Dan was standing behind her, arms folded over a Bale's Fudge and Confectionery apron. 'Um, do you have a minute for a chat?'

Lucy nodded, muttering a sound which might have been a yes.

33

SPROUTS

'I just bumped into Tarquin,' he said. 'He told me you were over here. I heard you finished de facto second in the talent contest.'

'I already have a bathroom carpet,' she said. At Dan's look of confusion, she added, 'That was the prize.'

'I bet the winner was ecstatic.'

Lucy shrugged. 'Well, it might have gone down better if an older person had won. I'm afraid my dad is pretty limited on what he can offer as prizes.'

'He's helping to make this extravaganza a great success,' Dan said. 'That's the main thing.'

'Yeah, you're right. And he's having a great time. Although I'm not sure exactly what he's been doing. I haven't seen him all day.'

'Well, it's Christmas Eve, and the main concert doesn't start until nine. Dad said I could take the afternoon off since he's got me on duty every day from Boxing Day right through to New Year's Eve, and I'm pretty worn out after this morning's madness—'

'With, um, Elizabeth?'

'Well, she's quite something, isn't she?'

Lucy wondered if acting like a cat for the amusement of children was affecting her personality, as she felt a nearly uncontrollable urge to say something mean. Instead, she said simply, 'I heard you used to be an item. There must be something about her, mustn't there?'

Dan folded his arms—a defensive gesture? wondered Lucy's paranoid thoughts—and started to laugh. After a moment he shook his head.

'I was still in school when we were together,' he said. 'It was like, she's pretty, everyone else thinks I'm a nerd, and she's interested, so why not?' He shrugged. 'Look, I'd much rather discuss this over a turkey leg and a bowl of sprouts.'

'Sprouts?'

Dan poked a thumb back over his shoulder. 'That stall back there. It does bowls of sprouts with gravy. I mean, I'll take a turkey leg if they've got one, but sprouts are all you really need, aren't they?'

'Are you serious? You like sprouts?'

Dan gave a wistful grin. 'When I was a kid Mum used to buy them wholesale. Apparently until I was nine I wouldn't eat anything else on a Sunday. Mum reckoned I ended up with these shoulders because I ate so much iron when I was a kid.'

Lucy shook her head in disbelief. 'I've never met

anyone who could do little more than tolerate sprouts. We always have them for Christmas dinner, but it's a symbolic gesture.'

Dan beamed. 'Did you know there are more than a hundred and ten varieties?'

'Um, no … I'm pretty sure there is literally no one anywhere who actually knows that.'

Dan shook his head. 'They're the unappreciated super-vegetable. Tons of vitamins and minerals, energy-giving, immune-system-boosting … I used to eat a plateful after a surf because they're great for exhaustion. And good for your general health, too. They have anti-cancer agents, they ease constipation—'

Lucy threw up a hand. 'Look, I really don't need to know that. I'll humour you with a bowl, though. Since it is Christmas.'

She followed him over to the stall where Dan, bouncing up and down like an excited child, ordered two large bowls of sprouts with gravy and a couple of glasses of eggnog to wash them down. The combination was ghastly, but Dan wore a grin so wide Lucy thought she could have lifted the top of his head clean off.

'I know they come from Belgium, but can you believe that China is the biggest sprouts producer?' Dan said, spearing three on a plastic fork and jamming them into his mouth.

'Look, just shut up about sprouts,' Lucy said, unable to hide a grin. Could she really be having a conversation about sprouts with the surf-lifesaving, volunteer coastguard, professional dentist heir to a fudge empire? 'I mean, you said you were a nerd, but I thought you were joking.'

Dan shook his head. 'Nope.'

'But … the surfing? The coastguard work?'

Dan shrugged. 'It's all just compensation, isn't it? I mean, I grew up in a surfing village, and all my mates were surfers, so you know, I just kind of got into it. And I like helping people. It's just that, from an early age, I was obsessed with teeth.'

'Tarquin told me about the kids in the children's home.'

Dan rolled his eyes. 'Did he now? Yeah, that was one reason, but it wasn't the only one. I remember there was a kid at school with an underbite and he used to get harassed about it. Instead of joining in with making his life hell like you were supposed to and all that, I started thinking about how horrible it was that he was getting harassed for something about his appearance. I wanted to fix him rather than torment him.'

'So you got into dentistry?'

Dan smiled. 'Yeah. And after I qualified I went on to become an orthodontist. I still do community dental work in Bristol, but privately I specialise in fixing bites, problems with the way teeth line up, that kind of thing. Dad always calls me a dentist because it's less of a mouthful.'

'What happened to the guy with the underbite?'

Dan smiled. 'I caught up with him a few years after I qualified, and offered to fix it. He'd kind of got over it by then, but it's not all about putting up with a bit of teasing at school. It can cause jaw and neck pain in later life.'

Lucy smiled. 'And I'm sure you'd tell me all about it if I let you.'

'I would, but it tends to bore people. Elizabeth, in case you're wondering, couldn't stand it. She found my collection of dentistry magazines one day and it just exploded her concept of cool. She told me to throw them away. I refused.'

'So why's she all over you now?'

'Is that what this is all about?'

Lucy was feeling a tingle from the alcohol in the eggnog, and her tongue was loosening. It was Christmas, so she figured what the hell. Let it all out. She opened her mouth to tell him that she thought that, despite the obvious nerdisms, he was rather nice, and that she was genuinely enjoying his company … and that he if wanted to talk to her more about mouths and teeth and jawbones she would be quite happy to let him do it—

But none of that would come out. Instead, she said, 'Um … Tarquin's worried she's after you.'

'Tarquin's worried?'

'Yes. I mean, she, um, kissed you—'

Dan laughed. 'That was horrible, wasn't it? And then she started posting all that stuff on the internet. You know it's all a show, don't you? I suspected she was faking it, but Elizabeth has always been Tintagel's greatest drama queen. I told her back off once her photographers had stopped clicking away, but she was too busy preening to even notice. She's got no interest in me, just like she has no interest in Tintagel. For a while we both just serve her purpose.'

'Well, I suppose that's a relief.' Lucy stared at him, then realised she was staring at him, and stuffed a sprout into her mouth. It was harder than the ones Valerie always overboiled and she found her cheeks puffing out beaverishly as she tried to get it down.

Dan was staring back at her, an amused little smirk on his face. 'So, tell me,' he said, his voice lowering just a touch to make Lucy feel gooey inside. 'What makes you tick? You remind me of the guy with the underbite—not because of how he looked, of course; in fact I think you look rather nice—but because of what you're hiding behind.'

Lucy was too enraptured with the comment about her looking nice that she couldn't really remember what else he had said.

'The laugh?'

'Oh, that.'

'I think it's endearing.'

'You what?'

'I don't know why you don't laugh more. I can tell just from what Tarquin's said and what I've seen for myself that it holds you back in everything. Don't let it.'

'It doesn't hold me back. I just don't like laughing, that's all.'

Dan leaned forward. 'Well, as I was going to say before, if you're not busy between now and the concert, why don't we go and get something to eat? I know a nice little restaurant which is really relaxing, and if we go early enough we'll beat the crowds.'

Was he inviting her out to dinner? Somewhere pretty, somewhere quiet, where they could be alone?

There was only one word she needed to say. But as she readied the courage to say it, she heard her mother's voice from behind her.

'Lucy, there you are, I've been looking all over. Quick, can you come with me? It's your father. I'm afraid I think he's gone quite mad.'

34

PRESENTS

'He's obsessed with Brussel's sprouts,' Lucy said as she trailed Valerie through the snow. 'Did you know there are a hundred and ten varieties?'

Valerie glanced back over her shoulder. 'And I imagine they all taste exactly the same. What's up with you? You sound besotted.'

Lucy coughed, startling a couple of elderly people helping each other along the pavement. 'He said he likes my laugh. He called it endearing.'

'Well, I suppose that means his car's safe,' Valerie said with a smirk.

'Oh, Mum, I hope that was a joke.'

'Dear, of course it was. I'm happy for you. I hope I didn't interrupt anything.'

Lucy felt a pang of regret, but quickly let her memory of Tarquin's words, and seeing Mark by his wife's grave, extinguish it. Dan, if he really liked her, could wait another couple of hours while she helped prevent whatever family crisis had suddenly occurred.

'Um, not really. Just, well, we were going to get dinner.'

'Oh, dear, I'm sorry. Don't worry, I'm sure he'll understand. I just need someone to help talk your father around. He just won't see sense.'

They reached the entrance to the holiday park and found Theresa out at the top of the farm lane swishing a broom to clear a path through the snow.

'Merry Christmas,' she snapped. 'The time of the year for charity, isn't it? Couldn't you spare five minutes of your precious time to help an old lady clear a road? Or are you too busy eating and drinking like the rest of the louts?'

'When I asked you before—'

'Don't question me, girl.' Theresa kicked at the snow which puffed up into the air. 'We're approaching a fifty year high.'

Lucy shared a glance with Valerie, who gave a terse nod. 'You go on,' she said to Lucy. 'I'll help Theresa.'

The air seemed to grow still. Theresa had stood up straight, her broom held across her chest like a weapon. Lucy glanced at Valerie, who was wilting under Theresa's gaze like a flower dying in the sun. Valerie, not present at karaoke, couldn't possibly have known the severity of the crime she had just committed by pronouncing the holiday park owner's name with a hard T. She was beginning to understand the punishment though, as Theresa, unblinking, glared at Valerie with eyes so wide Lucy wouldn't have been surprised if lasers had come blasting out to fry her mother where she stood.

Fearing for her mother's safety, Lucy cleared her throat and said, 'Um, my dad was saying how he'd love to give you a newly fitted living room carpet as a present and thanks for your courtesy during our stay. Would you prefer blue or green?'

Theresa swung toward her. 'Black,' she growled. 'The darkest shade you have.'

'I'm sure it could be arranged.'

A slow smile spread over Theresa's face. 'What a lovely present,' she said.

The hold appeared to have been broken. 'Mum,' Lucy said, 'were you aware that Theresa used to be a professional singer?'

Valerie, giving Lucy a brief understanding nod at Lucy's emphasised pronunciation, smiled.

'Oh really? I'd love to hear you sing.'

'Then let's get back to work,' Theresa said. 'Broom over there.'

She nodded back over her shoulder at a broom lying in the snow against the hedge, perhaps brought with her for the very purpose of snaring some unsuspecting helper. Lucy gave Valerie a pat on the shoulder, then headed on down into the holiday park as the sound of Theresa's singing began. It was much better than her stare, Lucy thought, even if she didn't care much for the music.

Alan was standing outside their tent beside a van with Drake's Carpets written on the side. Craig, one of her father's staff, was standing with his hands on his hips as Alan turned a bathmat with a reindeer design over in his hands. Also present were Denzil Porthleven and Col from the surf club.

'What's up?' Lucy asked, nodding to the van. Inside were a couple of dozen stacked boxes. One was open, revealing dozens of Christmas-wrapped presents inside.

'I'm sure there's nothing to worry about,' Denzil said. 'I mean, I was thinking of something a little more age-appropriate, but who wouldn't want a nice new bathmat?'

'What's all this about?' Lucy asked.

Alan rolled his eyes. 'Your mother seemed to think that the kids wouldn't like these presents,' he said. 'Almost as soon as Craig arrived she went off on one.'

'Wait a minute, what presents? What kids?'

Alan exchanged a glance with Denzil. 'Well, it was supposed to be a surprise, but I suppose the cat's out of the bag now.'

'What cat? What bag? Dad, what are you talking about?'

Denzil patted Alan on the shoulder. 'Meet Father Christmas,' he said.

'*What?*'

'Your dad's kindly agreed to be the inaugural Father Christmas at tonight's closing event,' Denzil said. 'We're all set to go with the reindeer and sleigh. And these are the presents. There should be enough for all of the kids.'

'I hope so,' Alan said. 'There are two hundred of

them in there. Enough for half of North Cornwall, I expect.' He turned to Lucy. 'Your mother was just complaining about what they are. But it's Christmas. The thought's what counts, isn't it? And it's a bit late now to be going and changing everything.'

'I'm sure the little tykes will be delighted,' Denzil said, nodding his head to disguise the uncertainty in his eyes.

Lucy laughed. 'Denzil, you don't have to humour him because he's the main sponsor. Dad, the kids will hate these. No offense, but what kid wants to get a bathmat from Father Christmas?'

Alan frowned. 'Frances, can I have a word in private?'

Lucy winced. 'Sure, but only if you promise to call me Lucy. Make it a New Year's resolution.'

Alan grimaced. 'All right, I'll try.'

After telling Craig and Denzil to get some coffee from the tent, he led Lucy a little way down the road until they were out of earshot. As soon as he was certain they couldn't be overheard, he let out a gasp of frustration.

'Love, I completely forgot I was supposed to be providing presents for the kids until Denzil mentioned it last night. I had no idea what to do, but we had all this stock left over from last year. I gave Craig in the Bristol office a call and offered him double time to go in and wrap them all up then drive down here. It's all I could do.' He wiped sweat off his brow. 'You must think I'm a complete failure.'

'You know I would never think that,' Lucy said.

She tugged her bottom lip and frowned. 'Dad, when's the sleigh supposed to arrive at the cricket ground?'

'Right at the end of the concert. About ten. It's five o'clock now, and we're supposed to be setting off on a loop of the local area about nine. That's four hours. We don't have time to prepare any other presents. Not a couple of hundred of them at any rate.'

Alan's cheeks had reddened and Lucy feared for a moment that her dad would start to cry. She patted him on the arm.

'Don't worry, Dad. Maybe some of the kids will like them.'

Alan sighed. 'Even if they did, a lot of the kids are from local children's homes. How many bathmats can they possibly need? If there was time we could nip into town and just get some selection boxes or something, but all the shops will be shut on Christmas Eve.'

'Isn't there a supermarket or something around here?'

Alan shook his head. 'I suppose there might be a newsagent or something up the road which is still open, but it's unlikely to have two hundred boxes of chocolate or fudge, is it?'

'Fudge!' Lucy clicked her fingers. 'Dad, we're totally overthinking this. Come on, I have an idea. Bring Craig, Col, and Denzil. I think we're going to need all hands on deck for this one.'

Lucy explained her idea as they headed up to the main road. The others were skeptical, but Lucy was adamant it could be pulled off. At the top of the lane they found Valerie and Theresa still clearing snow.

'Mum, Theresa, come with us, please. We need your help.'

'What is it, dear?'

'We need people to help wrap presents for the kids.' She grinned at her dad. 'Father Christmas needs your help.'

Theresa leaned on her broom and scowled. 'Time for coffee and bed for me, girl.'

Lucy turned to her, offering the sweetest smile she could muster. 'But isn't Christmas the time for charity? And think of the children….'

'I used to school them,' Theresa said. 'I consider them rats. Don't I, Porthleven?'

Denzil couldn't look at her. 'Yes, Miss Theresa, Miss.'

'But since I'm in a good mood, I suppose I could spare a few of the precious seconds I have left in this horrible world.'

Lucy grinned. 'You'll forever be remembered as the woman who saved Christmas.'

'Oh, I hope not,' Theresa scowled, but fell into step anyway as Lucy led them down the high street to Bale's Fudge, where Klaus and Mark were outside, serving a line of people.

'We need fudge,' Lucy said. 'And pretty confectionery boxes. How many do you have?'

Mark lifted an eyebrow. 'How many do you need?'

'All of them. It's for the children.'

Just at that moment Tarquin appeared through

the door, holding a tray of fresh fudge. 'Here's the next batch,' he said.

'How much more have you got cooking back there?' Lucy asked. 'We need as much of it as you can make in the next hour.'

Mark shook his head. 'Even if we could make it that quick, it takes time to cool.'

'There must be a way,' Lucy said. 'We need it for the kids.'

Klaus lifted a hand. 'I suppose there is a way. It's rather unique….'

An hour later, Lucy was standing in the snow, leaning on a spade, when Alan came huffing out of the fudge shop's back door with a tray of fresh fudge in his hands.

'Next one,' he said.

Lucy pointed at a flat place she had made in the snow. 'Put it right there,' she said.

Alan dropped the tray. It immediately began to fizz and sink into the snow, so Lucy laid a sheet of tin foil over the top and then shoveled snow on top of it. The garden was now full of little mounds of snow where other trays lay buried.

'Good job,' she said.

'Do we have enough yet?'

'Tell them to keep cooking,' Lucy said. 'We need more.'

'We're running out of sugar,' Alan said. 'Klaus had to poach a couple of bags off the Castle Hotel.'

Lucy smiled. 'I don't think Elizabeth Trevellian will miss it on her cornflakes,' she said.

A gate in the fence opened and Tarquin appeared, pushing a wheelbarrow loaded with snow. 'Replenishments,' he said.

'Over there,' Lucy instructed. 'And I think we're ready to start digging up the first batches.'

Together, they cleared snow off the earliest trays. Tarquin poked a fork into a corner of the fudge and tried a piece. 'Soft in the middle, cold on the outside,' he said. 'Perfect snow-frozen caramel. It's definitely unique.'

They carried a few trays back into the shop, where Theresa sat with Valerie, assembling small confectionery boxes and cutting rolls of wrapping paper into squares.

'It's time to start cutting, packing and wrapping,' Lucy said. 'We have an hour to do two hundred.'

Half an hour later, Mark announced that they were out of sugar until he could get an emergency shipment down on Boxing Day morning. With Klaus left outside to man the stall, everyone else crowded into the shop to pack and wrap boxes of fudge.

'That's the last one,' Alan said, putting a fist-sized package into a cardboard box laden with more. He glanced round the circle at Lucy, Valerie, Mark, Theresa, Denzil, Craig, Col, and Tarquin.

'You guys are amazing,' he said. 'We couldn't have pulled this off without everyone here. What an effort.'

Valerie patted him on the back. 'Now it's over to you, dear. You'd better go and get your costume on.'

Everyone stood up, stretched their aching backs, and shook hands. Even Theresa offered a hint of a smile. Mark and Klaus offered to shut the stall for half an hour and help Alan carry the boxes of wrapped presents back to the holiday park. They offered to make sure Theresa got home safely, but the old woman muttered that since she was up here, she "might as well" have a walk around the cricket ground. Craig, Col, and Valerie decided to accompany her, while Denzil had to go back to the cricket ground too, in order to prepare to open the concert. Lucy started to follow Alan, Mark, and Klaus, but Tarquin put a hand on her arm.

'Oh no,' he said. 'You're coming with me. We have another job to do. We have to go and pick up the sleigh.'

35

ACCIDENT

BEFORE HEADING BACK TO THE CRICKET GROUND, Tarquin stopped at a drinks stall and bought them two steaming hot chocolates laden with marshmallows, to "perk us up a bit". Lucy was exhausted, and despite it being Christmas Eve, all she really wanted was a hot shower and an early night. When they reached the cricket ground, though, and found it crowded with people enjoying a series of Christmas-themed events and fairground rides, she realised she didn't need the hot chocolate at all. She felt like she'd never sleep again as long as she stayed here.

'It's magnificent,' she said, watching the hot air balloon, sparkling with Christmas lights, rise into the air. The children in the basket laughed with delight as the Christmas Extravaganza spread out below them. Over to the left, queues waited for hot dogs, hamburgers, cups of mulled wine, hot mince pies and portions of clotted-cream-covered Christmas puddings. In the centre, the merry-go-round, its top laden with snow, spun in a whirl of golden sparkles, while over on the stage, a local children's choir was singing a medley of Christmas classics. To her surprise, Lucy spotted Theresa sitting in the front row of the crowd, nodding and clapping along. Valerie, Col, and Craig, their work done for the evening, sat alongside her.

'Right, it's this way,' Tarquin said, leading Lucy through the crowd to a quiet area behind a line of stalls. The reindeer were already harnessed to the sleigh, and stood quietly waiting.

'It's all a bit dark and quiet,' Lucy said.

'It has lights, but we haven't turned them on yet,' Tarquin said. 'We're going to head back through the village to pick up your dad, then loop down into the valley and come up again at the end of the high street by the entrance to the Castle Hotel. There we'll turn on the lights and make a grand approach through the Christmas Market to the cricket ground, where Denzil should have everyone waiting.' He lifted a carrier bag. 'Put this on.'

Lucy frowned. 'What's this?'

'You can't come unless you're in costume,' he said.

'What costume?'

'Just put it on.'

'Don't worry,' came a voice out of the dark. 'We're all going to look ridiculous, so you'll fit right in.'

Lucy looked up. A shadow approached from

around the back of the sleigh. Its height made it clearly a man, but he wore skintight leggings under a tunic that was almost a skirt, with a pointed hat perched on his head. At first Lucy thought the costume was all black, and wondered what someone was doing in a Batman outfit at Christmas, but then he was caught in a shaft of light between two of the stalls and Lucy realised it was dark green.

'*Dan?* Why on earth are you dressed as Robin Hood?'

Dan rolled his eyes and grinned. 'I'm an elf,' he said.

Lucy couldn't help but laugh. She looked down in embarrassment and realised Dan was wearing Wellington boots over the tights, which in turn caused her to guffaw like a donkey drinking cola.

'Look, give it a rest or you'll scare the reindeer,' Dan said.

Had anyone else said it, Lucy might have been upset, but when she looked up and saw the grin on Dan's face, it only made her want to laugh more.

'Your dad wasn't the only one who forgot,' Tarquin said. 'Father Christmas needs his elves, doesn't he? We didn't have any spare costumes and unfortunately it was too late to order off the internet and get them delivered on time. I nipped down to Trago Mills this morning but they'd sold out of elf costumes and all I could get was a few Robin Hoods. They're green; they'll do.'

Dan grinned. 'And it'll be a bit dark,' he said. 'No one will notice.'

Lucy held up the bag. 'So what's in here?'

'We wanted you to be a fairy,' Tarquin said. 'All the Tinkerbells were in children's sizes so the best we could get was Maid Marian.'

Lucy grimaced. 'Gosh.'

Dan held up a string of fairy lights with a battery pack attached. 'Just hang these around your neck. Everyone will be watching your dad, anyway.'

Lucy started laughing again.

'Ow!' Dan flinched. 'Seriously, pack it in. Don just tried to bite me.'

'Don? Who's Don?'

Dan patted the closest reindeer on the nose as it nuzzled him. 'Donatella,' he said.

'That's the reindeer's name?'

Dan nodded. 'Don't ask. I didn't name them. We just have to drive the sleigh. Come on, get in. We have to go and pick up your dad. You can change in the back.'

Only as Lucy climbed in did she begin to wonder how exactly Dan knew how to drive a sleigh. 'Are you sure you know what you're doing?' she asked. 'I mean, I thought you were a dentist....'

Dan grinned. 'These reindeer aren't actually from Lapland,' he said. 'Ellie thought it would be fun to pretend, just to get everyone into the Christmas spirit. They're actually from Otterham Farm Park a few miles up the A39. I had a summer job there when I was in school, doing the sleigh rides around the park all day long. Denzil got my old boss to loan them on condition that I was put in charge. He was doing the rides through the village earlier, but he had to get back to his family tonight.' He grinned. 'I'm Father Christmas's official driver.'

'But … I doubt you had snow in summer, did you?'

Dan shrugged. 'My old boss said the reindeer got a bit skittish in the snow, because they're not used to it either, but as long as we go slowly we'll be fine.'

'I hope so.'

Tarquin pointed at his watch. 'Come on, we have get going or we'll be late.'

Lucy pulled on her costume while Tarquin climbed in beside Dan in the front. Dan glanced back over his shoulder and gave Lucy a smile that made her feel as soft inside as the marshmallows they had eaten on the way here.

'Don't watch,' she said, glaring at him. 'I want this costume to be a surprise.'

'I can't wait,' Dan said.

It turned out that the Maid Marian costume was basically a brown sack with a crown of plastic flowers. Even with the fairy lights strung around her waist, Lucy felt like a walking cardboard box. It was too late to find anything else, though, because they were already moving slowly through the streets, working their way through the tourists who wanted to take pictures of the reindeer. Dan grimaced at Tarquin, who just shrugged.

'A good job we left early,' he said, as they turned into the farm lane that led to the holiday park. With Dan struggling to control the reindeer in the snow, they made their way cautiously down to the courtyard outside Theresa's house, where they found a pile of presents covered with a tarpaulin.

'Where's your dad?' Tarquin asked.

Lucy looked around. A sleety line of footprints led back and forth between their tent and the courtyard.

'I'll go and look,' she said.

Climbing down from the sleigh, she made her way through the churned up snow. A light was on inside the tent, and she heard the sound of someone shuffling around.

'Dad? Are you in there?'

'Just a minute,' came his voice from inside. 'I'm just looking for an extra pillow or two.'

'What for?'

'Maximum effect.'

'Okay....'

'Right ... are you ready for this?'

'Go on then.'

'Step back from the terrace.'

Lucy did as she was told, climbing down off the steps onto the snow. It had begun to fall more heavily again now, filling up the areas people had cleared.

She looked up as the zip drew back on the tent flap.

'Ho, ho, ho....'

The door opened and Father Christmas stepped out, almost as wide as the doorway, a white beard hanging over his ample waist, his suit shining red and white as he lifted his arms to wave at an imaginary crowd, a bell jingling on the end of his hat. Lucy could only gasp, covering her mouth with her hands as the memory of ancient childhood delights threatened to make her squeal with excitement.

'How do I look?'

Lucy jumped up and down. 'Perfect!'

'Well, help me down off the steps. I can barely see in this thing, let alone figure out what my feet are doing.' A fluff-covered head tilted at her. 'What on earth are you wearing?'

'Long story,' she said, coming forward to help him down. 'I'm an, um, a Cornish fairy.'

Alan nodded. 'Oh, right … I suppose they looked that way back when Cornwall was all mines and farming. To blend in, I suppose. Minus the fairy lights, of course.'

Lucy smiled. 'Come on, we're all ready. The, um, elves are loading up the sleigh.'

She helped him through the snow, holding his arm to stop him slipping. Alan made as many "hos" as "woahs" as the snow threatened to steal his feet from under him. Finally, they reached where Dan and Tarquin stood, both breathing heavily as they leaned on the sleigh.

'Wow, two hundred bathmats work out pretty heavy,' Dan said. 'I thought you had decided to go with fudge instead? That's what Trev said.'

Alan shrugged. 'Waste not, want not. There might be some big kids among the audience who still want to sit on Father Christmas's knee.'

'And see just how much the magic of Christmas

has deteriorated over the years,' Lucy quipped, before bursting into spontaneous laughter.

'Remember what I said about scaring the reindeer?' Dan said, smiling as he patted her on the arm, a touch that sent shivers through her. Lucy tried to be quiet but only found herself laughing more, this time through nerves.

'Are we ready?' Tarquin said. 'The boys are ready to go.'

'They're all girls,' Dan reminded him. 'Male reindeer lose their antlers in winter. All Santa's reindeer would have had to have been girls.' With a smug grin, he patted the nearest on the side and it gave a snort in response. 'Ready, Mike?'

'Mike?' Lucy asked.

'Michaela.'

'Oh.'

With Tarquin at the front and Dan pushing from behind, they managed to lever Alan up onto the sleigh, where they positioned him to Dan's right with Tarquin and Lucy in the seats behind. The rest of the sleigh's space was filled with presents inside colourful sacks, all covered by a black tarpaulin to keep off the snow.

'Okay, off we go,' Dan said, flicking the reins.

The reindeer started into a brisk canter, the sleigh bouncing over the ground. Instead of heading up the farm lane back to the village, however, Dan turned left, heading down the track past Theresa's farmhouse and along a gloomy lane between two hedgerows that appeared as dark humps out of the night.

'This track connects with the valley road out that comes out by the Castle Hotel,' Dan said. 'Unfortunately, it's a bit dark.'

He slowed their pace until the reindeer were walking slowly as the last glow from the farmhouse's outside lights faded behind them. Dan reached underneath the seat and produced a battery lantern, which he switched on and passed to Lucy.

'Would you like to do the honour of leading the reindeer?' he asked. 'It's only a couple of hundred metres until we come out on the main road. There should be some street lighting there.'

Lucy nodded. 'Sure, why not?'

She pulled a Christmas hat down over her head in case anyone out in the dark saw her, then climbed down and walked past the reindeer to the front. The huge, shaggy creatures grunted and snorted as she passed, but with only the lamp's circular glow to light the world around her, she felt in the middle of a romantic Christmas wonderland. Behind the reindeer, in the shadows of the sleigh, sat Father Christmas and two elves, while in front of her was only a blanket of white, untouched snow. More pattered around her as the reindeer tossed their heads and tugged on their harnesses.

She began to walk forward, the snow rising halfway to her knees, the circle of light extending out in front of her. After a few steps she heard Dan flick the reins and the reindeer began to follow, the crunch of their hooves in the snow coupled with the squeak of the sleigh's runners. The road began to slope downhill. Dan angled the sleigh from side to side to slow its momentum, while Tarquin worked a mechanism in the back which acted as a brake. Soon, the road began to flatten out, and in the shadows up ahead, Lucy saw an opening where the lane joined a larger road.

From just out of sight came muffled voices.

Lucy turned back to the others and lifted a hand. 'Wait a minute,' she said. 'Something's going on out on the road. I'll go and check it out.'

Feeling an excited desire to keep their presence secret as long as possible, Lucy switched off the lamp and made her way forward, walking through the lighter shadows between the darker ones denoting the hedgerows. When she stepped out onto the main road, however, she saw Dan had been right: every twenty or thirty metres a street light rose out of the trees beside the road, marking the passage up to Tintagel.

The voices came again. Lucy stared. Below the nearest streetlight, pressed up against the hedgerow with a mound of snow foaming over its bonnet, was a crashed car. Nearby, three people stood in the snow, clearly in the midst of some kind of causality argument.

Lucy looked back again at the car and frowned.

It was a rather nice car, the only one of its kind Lucy had seen during her stay in Tintagel.

A Bentley.

36

RESCUE

'YOU SHOULDN'T HAVE BEEN DRIVING LIKE A maniac,' Elizabeth Trevellian snapped, then hit Shawn on the shoulder with a flat palm. 'Didn't you ever pass your driving test? What did you do, just make a fake one on the internet and print it out? If we ever get back to anywhere civilised you'll be heading for the unemployment queue.'

'I told you we should have put snow tyres on the thing,' Shawn replied.

'When there was no chance of snow? What a waste of time.'

'Shawn was probably right,' Peter said.

'You can shut up, too.'

'I hope it's insured.'

'It's a rental. Of course it's insured.'

Peter rolled his eyes. 'Perhaps you could set up a GoFundMe to get your fans to pay for the deductible,' he said, voice thick with sarcasm.

'Well, I will as soon as I can get reception for my phone,' Elizabeth snapped. 'If you had to crash, couldn't you have done it a little farther up the hill?'

'Would this be a good time to talk about Christmas bonuses?' Shawn said, grinning at Peter behind Elizabeth's back.

'Your bonus is that you get to work with me. How many people out there would literally pay for the privilege?'

'Perhaps you ought to post an online auction once you've dropped us off at the JobCentre,' Peter said. 'I'd be happy to give you a review. I doubt you can get better conversation anywhere.'

'What's that supposed to mean?'

'Nothing. Nothing at all.'

'Oh, can't you get us out of here?'

Shawn sighed. 'The front wheel's stuck in a storm drain. It probably only needs a good push. If all three of us were doing it....'

'I told you, these nails are fresh. I need them for the midnight shoot we're not going to miss thanks to your incompetence. Can't you hike back up to the village and find some filthy local to help? Go on, I'll wait in the car.'

As she went to open the back door, Lucy stepped out of the shadows from where she had been enjoying the conversation.

'Merry Christmas,' she called. 'Would you like some help? I have a few friends just up that lane who I'm sure wouldn't mind giving you a push.' She smiled. 'Not if it would help you get on your way a little quicker.'

Elizabeth had been frowning, but now her eyes widened as she recognised Lucy.

'Oh my, it's you. The Beast. Quick, Shawn, get the camera. I told you she was stalking me. This must be a criminal offence. Did you cause this? Did you make my car crash just to ruin my Christmas? What are you, some sort of witch? I mean, you're dressed like a potato, but I suppose that's just a disguise.'

Lucy smiled. 'If I had the power to crash cars I'd probably put it to better use. Would you like some help or not?'

Elizabeth huffed and climbed into the car, slamming the door.

'Yes, please,' Peter said, while Shawn glanced at Elizabeth and rolled his eyes.

Lucy called up the lane to Dan, who moved the sleigh forward. Both Peter and Shawn let out surprised gasps as first the reindeer, then the laden sleigh with its jovial Father Christmas, appeared out of the narrow lane entrance.

'We've got some rope in the back,' Tarquin called. 'Does that thing have a tow bar? We could easily pull you out. Got six reindeer-power to work with.'

Peter and Shawn were still staring. As Lucy watched their shocked expressions with a bemused smile, the back door opened and Elizabeth climbed out.

'Dan?' she said, seemingly oblivious to the

magnificent reindeer. 'Is that you? Wow, you look ridiculous.'

'Lovely to see you, too,' Dan called down. In the back, Tarquin was grinding his teeth to keep the insults inside, while behind the huge beard, there was no clue as to what Alan thought of everything.

'Can you kindly give us a pull?' Shawn said. 'We'd very much appreciate it. These roads are treacherous at the best of times, but this snow....'

'Sure,' Dan said. He turned around and waved to Tarquin, who jumped down with a coil of rope, giving Elizabeth a wide berth as she came forward.

'Dan, it's Christmas Eve,' Elizabeth said, pushing past the reindeer and peering up at him. 'There's still time to be my Christmas romance for this year. Come on, my followers would love it.'

'You must be joking,' Dan said. 'I think I'd rather be Theresa's.'

'Do I look like I'm joking?' Elizabeth said, stamping her foot. 'This is your last chance, Dan. I won't come looking for you again. Once you're set adrift, you're adrift for good.'

'Can we just get the car out first before we have any little lovers' tiffs?' Shawn said. 'It's freezing and if no one has noticed, it's still snowing.'

Dan seemed happy to urge the reindeer on, leaving Elizabeth standing in the road behind. Tarquin jumped out of the back and, after giving Elizabeth a catty air-claw with his hand, helped Peter tie the rope around the Bentley's tow bar.

'That's it,' Tarquin said, standing up. 'Right, if we

all give it a push and a lift from the front, the sleigh should be able to drag it out.'

Dan positioned the sleigh slightly uphill from the stuck Bentley, moving the reindeer forward until the rope went taut. Lucy, Tarquin, Peter, and Shawn got into position around the car, with only Alan, stuck in place as a bemused Father Christmas, and Elizabeth, standing in the road with her hands on her hips, doing nothing.

'On three,' Dan said. 'One, two, three … push!'

The sleigh shook, bumping a little off the ground. The Bentley inched back a little way, but remained stuck. Dan called a halt and turned to Elizabeth.

'Get in and start the engine,' he said. 'The wheels might be able to grip now, so put it into reverse and wait for the signal.'

Huffing as though being asked to climb a mountain, Elizabeth did as she was instructed. She started the engine and wound the front window down, glaring at Dan as snow melted in her hair.

'Okay, once more,' Dan shouted. 'Ready …. push!'

This time the wheels came free with a groan of the engine and a spray of snow.

'Thanks, guys,' Shawn said, turning to the others. 'We thought we'd be stuck there all night.'

'Saved by Father Christmas, who'd have thought it?' Peter added. 'It's been quite a night. I suppose we'd better get on our way, make sure Madam makes her midnight photo shoot.'

He reached for the back door, but the automatic

locks clicked, and the handle worked uselessly. Elizabeth leaned out of the open driver's front window.

'You're fired, both of you,' she snapped. 'Merry Christmas.'

'Hang on, wait a minute—' Shawn began, but Elizabeth tossed a camera case out on the ground, making him jump back.

'Here's your present. There will be better photographers than you there tonight and I'm getting sick of your whining. Don't you understand how lucky you are?'

'You're such a snob,' Tarquin said.

'And you're such a … oh, I don't know where to start. Are you sure your father didn't have an affair? I mean, your brother's such a dish, but you—'

'Leave him alone,' Lucy said.

'Or what, you'll *laugh* at me?' As Lucy scowled, Elizabeth leaned out of the car and waved to Dan, her expression switching as though her face were a slide projector clearing out the dust. 'Dan, why don't you ditch these losers and come with me? It's Christmas Eve, the most romantic time of the year. Wouldn't you love to be beside me when the clock chimes midnight?'

Dan laughed. 'I'd rather be lying between two of these reindeer,' Dan said. 'After they've had a bucket of sprouts each.'

'Brutal,' Tarquin said, clicking his fingers.

'Oh, you and your sprouts. Honestly, sometimes I think you're as big a loser as your brother. Well, have it your way. I'm done with you country bumpkins.' As she leaned back into the car, she glanced at Lucy. 'You have a nice evening, Beast. Don't scare too many people.'

'Wait!'

Lucy, who, on one level, was enjoying the cartoon-like absurdity of Elizabeth's tantrum, looked up to see Alan climbing down out of the sleigh.

'Dad, what are you doing?'

'I'm not your dad, love, I'm Father Christmas. And I've got a little present for this wild young lady.'

'What are you talking about?' Elizabeth snapped.

Alan as Father Christmas held up a little present. 'This is for you,' he said, reaching into the Bentley and holding it out for Elizabeth to reach out and take. 'Merry Christmas, young lady. I hope you overcome whatever traumas you're suffering and have a good one.'

Elizabeth's expression had changed once again, and now she appeared genuinely touched as she turned the square present over in her hands.

'Um, I don't know what to say. That's very kind of you, um, Father Christmas.'

'You have a nice Christmas now,' Father Christmas said, patting the side of the Bentley with one white-gloved hand. 'And drive carefully on these roads. We're going back into the village, so we won't be able to pull you out again. And I don't care how rich you are, breakdown services will charge a fortune to come out on Christmas Eve.'

Elizabeth gave him a sweet smile. 'Well, thank you very much.'

'My pleasure.'

With one last nod, Father Christmas headed back to his sleigh. Dan helped him climb back up while the others stood around as Elizabeth lined the car up and pointed it downhill. She leaned out of the window, looking as though she would throw out some last insult, but instead she just said, 'Well, Merry Christmas,' and then sped off down the road, driving far faster than was probably safe, the Bentley bumping through tracks carved in the snow by other traffic.

'Well, I suppose that's that,' Shawn said, turning to Peter. 'Do you think they'll have any vacancies left at that hotel?'

'They might not,' Alan called down, 'but if you don't mind roughing it a bit, I'm sure we could find room for you in the tent.'

'That would be very kind of you,' Peter said. 'Much as I enjoyed the money, she was never the easiest person to work for.'

'You got off lightly,' Dan called down. 'I used to go out with her. It used to take her two hours to get ready just for a walk up to the chip shop. I still get nightmares fifteen years later.'

'I don't suppose we could get a lift back up to the village?' Shawn asked.

Tarquin climbed up into the back of the sleigh and rummaged under one of the seats. 'You can do more than that,' he said, tossing them both a carrier bag. 'I have a couple of spare costumes. You might as well look the part.'

'How many did you buy?' Dan asked, frowning.

Tarquin shrugged. 'It was Trago Mills, and you know what that place is like. I figured if I didn't buy them when I saw them, I'd never see them again.'

Peter and Shawn climbed up into the back of the sleigh. Dan reached down to help Lucy up, but as she moved to climb into the back he shook his head and slid over. 'You can sit up the front if you like,' he said.

Lucy felt another little flutter, but she swallowed it down. After all, her dad was only a couple of feet away, on Dan's other side. To hide her excitement, she said, 'Dad, that was nice of you to give her a present. What was it?'

Alan shrugged. 'One of those old bathmats,' he said. 'I figured we might as well start getting rid of them. Right, is everyone ready?' A cheer came from the back. 'Then I think it's time we got the lights on and brought Christmas to this little Cornish village.'

37

GRAND ARRIVAL

'I FEEL A LITTLE SORRY FOR ELIZABETH,' LUCY SAID, as the sleigh moved, the rows of fairy lights that covered it so bright she had to squint at the cheering crowds that lined the street. 'I mean, she's all alone on Christmas.'

'Do you really think Elizabeth's alone?' Dan said. 'She's not alone. She has her fifty million or whatever social media followers. That's all she really cares about. Even when I was briefly stupid enough to go out with her, she was obsessed with what complete strangers thought about her. It was no surprise that she's a top model, but she's welcome to all her money and fame. I'd rather be here, riding on this sleigh, sitting between Father Christmas and Maid Marian.' He gave her hand a light squeeze. 'Merry Christmas, Lucy.'

'Are you making a move on my daughter, young

man?' Alan said, huge beard swinging around. 'Don't forget I'm right here.'

'Dad, please, I'm a grown woman,' Lucy muttered, wishing she had a spare piece of sacking to pull over her head as amused sniggers came from the seats behind them.

'You're still my little girl,' Alan said. 'You're still my little Frances Drake.'

'Oh, please just call me Lucy,' she said, but Dan lifted a hand.

'Well, since I'm in the position of sitting next to this wonderful girl's father,' he said, 'could I take the opportunity to ask her father's permission to take her out on a date?'

'How romantic,' Tarquin said from the back, clapping his hands together.

Alan laughed. 'Granted, young man. Father Christmas gives his approval. Where are you going?'

Dan shrugged. 'Well, I was thinking the Eden Project. It has a special Boxing Day event going on.'

'Really? Val and I have always wanted to go there. Perhaps we could all go.' Alan nudged Lucy in the ribs. 'It would be like a double date. Wouldn't that be nice?'

'Fantastic,' Lucy muttered.

'Is that zip line open in winter?'

'The zip line? I'm not sure—'

'Dad, no way Mum would let you near that. It probably has an upper weight limit anyway.'

'But it's Christmas!'

Lucy had no more time to think about her

upcoming date with Dan and her parents, because the sleigh had reached the turning into the cricket ground. To triumphant cheers, Dan urged the reindeer forward into a cordoned off space in front of the stage, just as a man in a mirrored top hat, flared trousers, and massive platform boots, and who looked vaguely familiar, roared 'It's *Christmas!*' and the air filled with pieces of glitter that rained down on the cheering crowd.

As four men in shiny costumes lifted their instruments and waved to the crowd before walking off, Denzil made his way to the centre of the stage. He picked a bit of tinsel off the microphone, and then shouted, 'Slade, everyone!' to another raucous cheer.

'Was that really Slade?' Dan asked Lucy. 'They looked a bit young.'

Alan huffed. 'Of course they do. They're ageless,' he said. 'Like a fine wine.'

'And now, it's time to meet the main man of the event,' Denzil shouted. From the glow of his cheeks it was obvious he'd been on the sherry backstage. 'Give it up for Mr. Father Christmas himself!'

'Stand up and wave, Dad!' Lucy hissed as people began to cheer again, moving as close as they could to the sleigh, pressing against a temporary fence staffed by a line of people in Christmas hats. Alan, holding on to Dan for support, shakily got to his feet. 'Merry Christmas!' he bellowed, waving at the crowd. As Lucy scanned the adoring faces, it became immediately obvious that there were far more than two hundred kids likely to line up for a present. Lucy nudged Dan, who turned in the seat to look at Tarquin. Squatting down in the sleigh so he wouldn't be seen, Tarquin pulled out his phone.

'Speech, speech!' came the cry from the crowd. Alan gave an uncomfortable shrug, but Denzil had climbed down from the stage, the microphone in hand.

'Welcome to Tintagel,' he said as he reached the sleigh and held up the microphone. 'We're very glad to have you here with us tonight. It must have been quite a journey all the way from the North Pole.'

Alan leaned down to speak into the microphone. 'That it was,' he said. 'Quite a journey indeed. We even had to stop to help a damsel in distress on the way. But we made it, and we are glad to be here. Regardless of what you believe, Christmas is a time to be happy, let your hair down—or what hair you have left—and have a good time.'

The crowd cheered. 'Is it true that you've got something for the children in the crowd, Father Christmas?' Denzil asked.

'That's right. What would Christmas be without presents? On my sleigh here, I have something for the little ones, and also something for the parents too … while stocks last.'

More cheers, but mostly from the children. The parents looked a little skeptical, but most were probably too full on mince pies and mulled wine to care much about presents.

Denzil helped Father Christmas down off the sleigh and over to the stage. Lucy smiled as her father, overloaded with beard, struggled with his footing through the slush in front of the stage while simultaneously waving at the crowd. She wasn't the only one living out a childhood fantasy, she realised.

Staff had dragged an armchair with Tintagel Cricket Club written on the back into the centre of the stage. Denzil helped Alan to sit down, the lack of springs making him chuckle as his legs kicked up into the air.

As Alan got himself comfortable, the four elves and Lucy—getting a few odd looks from the crowd— carried the colourful sacks of presents over to the stage side. Alan propped himself up on some hastily provided cushions while Denzil arranged the children into a line. When Alan was settled, he instructed them to make their way up on to the stage one by one.

The sacks of presents quickly began to empty as the children came to sit on a deckchair beside Alan, answered a couple of questions, took a present and left. Tarquin kept looking at his watch, his expression increasingly agitated. Ten p.m. and then eleven came and went, and yet the line still seemed without end. They were on the last box when suddenly Mark came hurrying out of the backstage area with a cardboard box in his hands, followed by Klaus and a couple of other men Lucy didn't recognise.

'We got it,' he said to Tarquin. 'Called up the lads from the fudge shops in Boscastle and Padstow and got you some relief. North Cornwall will be fudge-free on Christmas Day, but then I suppose we all need a day off.'

'Thanks, Dad.'

The supply was more than enough. As the last few children made their way onto the stage, some of them yawning as midnight approached, Valerie began helping a number of older people up to the stage side. Lucy grinned.

'Dad'll be delighted to shift a few of those bathmats,' she said to Dan. 'It looks like it'll be a successful Christmas all round.'

Dan grinned. 'Listen, I think we're about finished here. There's something else I have to do, out on the clifftop. Would you, um, like to come along?'

Lucy could barely speak. Was Dan trying to get her alone? Then she remembered: she had promised to take part in Frederika's yodeling chorus performance. It had almost slipped her mind, but it was due to start right after Father Christmas departed, part of the closing ceremony for the night.

'Um, I have to, um, yodel.'

'I know. It says it on the revised itinerary.'

'It does?'

Dan pulled a leaflet out of his pocket and unfolded it. At the bottom, beneath *Meet Father Christmas!* it said, *Swiss Yodeling Chorus, featuring internet sensation, Lucy "Cat Lady" Drake.*

'Oh.'

'You can't miss it, because that's what half of the crowd has come to see,' Dan said, grinning. 'Father Christmas is so last millennium. No pressure, eh? Don't worry, I had a word with Frederika. She doesn't mind if you're a bit late. You're the main attraction, so it'll help build some anticipation if you're not on time.'

'You've already spoken to her?'

Dan shrugged. 'I bumped into her earlier. I hope you don't mind.'

Lucy beamed. 'No problem. Well, let's go then.'

The children, tired but glowing with excitement as they stuffed fudge into their mouths, had made way for a free-for-all of parents and older people giving Father Christmas a quick shake of the hand before taking a wrapped bathmat out of the last couple of bags. Denzil stood at Alan's shoulder with the microphone, and during a brief moment between well-wishers, he leaned down and said, 'Christmas Day is nearly upon us. Father Christmas, will you stay to give us a countdown?'

'I certainly will,' Alan said, his voice sounding hoarse from too many bellows of "ho-ho-ho". Valerie, helping to hand out presents, gave Alan a surreptitious pat on the knee, then looked over to where Lucy waited at the stage side and smiled. With a brief tilt of her head and a raised eyebrow, she told Lucy what she should do.

Leaving Tarquin, Shawn, and Peter to finish up the elf duties, Lucy and Dan slipped away across the cricket field, past several stalls now closed up for the night and a dark big top similarly empty. They crunched through untouched snow to the boundary edge, where Dan led Lucy through a gate now hung with fairy lights and down a path between two fields toward the clifftop and the coast path. He illuminated their way with a pocket torch, but as they reached the intersection with the coast path, he turned to Lucy and switched it off.

Lucy realised the snow had stopped, and the moon hung in a clear sky. As her eyes adjusted, she could make out Dan in front of her standing amidst a winter wonderland. A short way behind him, the cliff edge was fenced off, and beyond it, the choppy sea rolled and toiled. Over the village of Tintagel, the lights of the Christmas Extravaganza lit up the night sky.

Dan pulled his phone out of his pocket and checked the time. Then, slipping it back into his pocket, he sighed and looked up at her. 'We made it,' he said. 'Just in time.'

'In time for what?'

He reached out for her hand and turned her toward the sea. 'Look,' he said.

'At what? The sea? It's pretty, I suppose—'

'The horizon,' Dan said. 'Can you see the lights?'

Lucy stared. As her eyes adjusted, they appeared, a string of dots along the horizon.

'Merchant ships,' Dan said. 'At midnight on Christmas Eve, they all start flashing their lights. It's like a tradition. When I was a kid, I used to come out here every year to watch it.'

From somewhere behind came the ring of a church bell, and slightly fainter, a gravelly, hoarse voice counting down from ten as people cheered.

'That's it,' Dan said.

As though able to hear the cue, the line of lights

stretching as far as Lucy could see began to twinkle on and off. She stared as the entire horizon became a single string of fairy lights.

'It must be hard for them out there at this time of year,' Dan said. 'Away from their families and friends. We're lucky, aren't we?'

Without realising it, Lucy found Dan's arm around her shoulder. She leaned in against him, enjoying the warmth of his body.

'You know, while I think you have a lovely smile, and there's really nothing wrong with your teeth that I can see at all, I wouldn't mind it one little bit if you found some reason to stop by my dental practice once you're back in Bristol,' Dan said.

Lucy gulped. Her hands felt clammy, her throat dry. 'Maybe I could drop off some travel brochures or something,' she croaked.

'That would be great,' Dan said.

His face was close to hers. Lucy wasn't sure how it had got there, but it was right in front of her, glowing in the moonlight. She felt his lips brush hers, felt the tickle of his breath.

'Merry Christmas, Lucy,' Dan said.

'Merry Christmas,' she replied, letting him pull her close, as the pop and crackle of fireworks came from the cricket ground. They turned to look, holding on to each other, as sparkling lights exploded into the night sky.

END

AFTERWORD

To all my readers, thank you so much for your support over the years. It means a lot. I hope you will enjoy this book as much as all the others.

To the residents of Tintagel, Cornwall, I did play around with the geography a little bit, changed names, added shops and pubs, and generally turned your village upside down. I hope you don't mind. As someone who spent many a summer evening playing evening league cricket on your fine cricket ground, as well as eating fudge and pasties from your many wonderful shops, I hope you'll forgive me. If, however, this book inspires you to create a real life Christmas Extravaganza, I would be delighted to attend.

CPW

September, 2019

ACKNOWLEDGMENTS

Big thanks as always to those of you who provided help and encouragement. A special thanks to Elizabeth for the cover and to Jenny Twist, for your eternal support.

In addition, extra thanks goes to my Patreon supporters, in particular to Amaranth Dawe, Ann Bryant, Janet Hodgson, Leigh McEwan, James Edward Lee, Catherine Crispin, Alan MacDonald, Eda Ridgeway, Jennie Brown, Nancy, and Norma.

You guys are awesome.

ABOUT THE AUTHOR

CP Ward loves writing Christmas books. This is his second attempt, after last year's well-received *I'm Glad I Found you this Christmas*. There will be more...

There might be more ...

Chris would love to hear from you:
chrisward@amillionmilesfromanywhere.net

Made in the USA
Monee, IL
13 October 2021